Travel
Far,
Pay No
Fare

Travel Far, Pay No Fare

Anne Lindbergh

Osprey Press

For the children at Riverside School,
who went inside this story
and changed a few things

VERMONT
SUMMER
READING
MARATHON

Travel far,
Pay no fare,
Let a story
Take you there!

⇢⇢ *One* ⇠⇠

A COUPLE OF YEARS AGO when I was ten, my dad left home for the umpteenth time and stayed away. It was kind of a relief. By then I had learned not to get my hopes up each time he came back. Also that my mom and I could get on fine alone. So I didn't panic when Dad said, "Owen—take care of Mom— she'll need it!" I just said, "Okay."

And that's what I did for two whole years after the divorce: I took care of my mom. She did the parenting, of course. Don't get the idea that she neglected me or anything like that. She fed me and fussed over me, and went to teacher conferences at school—it's just that I had to tell her *when* to do these things, because her head was in the air. She's a writer.

My mom is Nan-Ellen Noonan. For most people, that name rings a bell: It's printed on the covers of thirty books for children. She has been turning them out at the rate of two a year since long before I was born. All thirty of those books are about kids with problems. That sounds depressing, but it's not, because the kids are funny and their problems are too. I don't know how Nan-Ellen thinks them up. They're certainly not inspired by me; I've always been too busy taking care of her to make her laugh.

Back home in Boston, I used to go along to the bookstores and help Nan-Ellen with her signings. I'd line the kids up, and make sure they had their books open to the right page, and so on. She paid me by the hour, which is how I saved enough to buy my own television set. I hated the job. As Nan-Ellen Noonan's son, I got asked too many questions.

"My favorite story is the one about the boy with forty-nine warts," some kid would say. "Was that supposed to be you?"

Then his mother would gush, "You're so lucky to be Nan-Ellen Noonan's son! I bet you're a big reader, aren't you?"

My answer was "no" to both questions. I didn't have warts, and I wasn't a big reader. When I wasn't keeping an eye on Nan-Ellen Noonan, I watched TV. Pretty soon I wised up and quit saying "Mom" in public. I trained myself to say "Nan-Ellen" instead. The habit spread to the privacy of our home and stuck. Even after we moved to Vermont, where everyone knew I was her son, we stayed on a first-name basis.

The reason for Vermont was Uncle Jack. He used to be married to Aunt Lyle, who was Nan-Ellen's sister, but she died a long time ago, leaving him with my cousin Parsley. Uncle Jack and Parsley lived in this really rural neighborhood that was a great place to visit when we needed a break from city life. A short break, not a permanent change. Nan-Ellen and I were both city people. I was, at least, and I took it for granted that she was too. That's why I got so upset when she broke the news to me last July.

I happened to be in my bedroom, watching *Star Trek: The Next Generation*. Just as the crew was being attacked by hostile Romulans, Nan-Ellen came in and blocked the screen. Of all the times to tell me that she was getting remarried!

"Live in Vermont?" I said. "You've got to be kidding! Uncle Jack only gets two channels."

"Channels?"

Nan-Ellen looked baffled, as if I were speaking a foreign language. It was just an act, though. She knew it did no good to bad-mouth television, so she pretended it didn't exist. The *Enterprise* was in trouble—I could tell by the sound effects. Why didn't she leave the room so I could go on watching?

"Only *one* channel, come to think of it," I said, craning my neck to see the screen behind her. "Three or eight, depending which way the wind blows. Whichever way, they don't get *Star Trek*."

Nan-Ellen smiled. "That's not much of an objection. Look at it like this: You may be losing the *Enterprise*, but you're gaining a father."

"I've already got a father," I reminded her. "Just because you divorced him doesn't mean he's dead. Besides, isn't it illegal to marry a relation?"

"Only when it's a blood relation," she said.

I didn't argue the point. It wasn't important anyway. What really mattered was that she had sprung this on me at the worst possible time. I loved Boston. I had a whole bunch of friends there. We were entering junior high that fall and really looking forward to it. Uncle Jack was a nice guy, in my opinion, but not nice enough to turn my life upside down. How could Nan-Ellen be so selfish?

When my dad disapproved of something, he didn't argue. Instead, he used to cross his arms and tilt his head to one side while he waited for you to change your mind. Now I tried it on Nan-Ellen, but it didn't work. She just smiled at me in this totally confident way, looking so much like the photo on her book flaps that it freaked me out. If you've read Nan-Ellen Noonan's stories, you must have noticed

4

that photo. She's a noticeable person. It's the look on her face more than anything else: kind of a happy, expectant look as if she thinks something great is about to happen. That evening she *knew* something great was about to happen. But did she know what a disaster it would be for me?

"We'd better take some time to think this over," I said.

"I *have* taken time," Nan-Ellen said. "Jack asked me to marry him ages ago, but I didn't want to rush things. I still don't. We'll drive up to Vermont at the end of August like every other summer, only this time we'll stay. No sudden changes; it will all seem natural."

"Natural for you, maybe."

"For you too. Believe me, I've given it a lot of thought."

"So when's the big fancy wedding?" I asked.

Nan-Ellen's answer was so smooth that I could tell she had planned it in advance. "It won't be big and fancy. We'd like a quiet ceremony out on the lawn, if the weather is nice. I thought we'd drive up on the twenty-ninth and have the wedding on the first of September. That's a Saturday."

"Great!" I said bitterly. Then I added, "Don't I have any choice in the matter?"

"Not about whether I marry Jack. It's my life, after all."

"It's mine too," I said.

I could hear my voice rising in anger, but I couldn't help it. "You're making me change schools, right? When I start seventh grade I won't know a soul, and when I come home after school there'll only be one channel to watch. But it's your life, right?"

"Calm down," Nan-Ellen advised me. "You'd be changing schools anyway, don't forget. And think what you gain—we'll be a real family again! One reason Jack and I are getting married is that it will be good for you and Parsley."

I didn't want Nan-Ellen to see my face until I got a handle on myself, so I zapped the TV with my remote control and went to the window to look out. Our apartment was on the eleventh floor. We had a panoramic view of air-conditioning vents like robot sentinels, keeping watch over roof gardens that gave green glimpses into other people's lives. I loved those gardens, although it didn't seem right to spy on people. That evening last July, one of the owners noticed me and waved. Embarrassed, I backed into the room.

"Parsley and I are already cousins," I said. "That's good enough."

"Now she'll be your sister too. Anyway, you look so much alike that strangers would believe it."

I groaned. "Thanks a bunch! Half the world has

brown hair. That doesn't mean I look like Parsley. By the way, did Uncle Jack bother to ask her if she wanted a brother?"

Nan-Ellen proceeded to explain how having a great kid like me for a big brother would bring warmth and confidence into Parsley's lonely life. I looked at her suspiciously. Sure enough, she was wearing her writer face—a distracted expression that meant she was busily turning fact into fiction. She had never used me as a character in one of her books and I was glad: It would have been an invasion of my privacy. But I have to admit I felt jealous at the thought that she might use Parsley.

"Parsley is a funny little thing!" Nan-Ellen concluded.

I said, "Parsley is boring."

That was a lie. Parsley wasn't boring; she was just weird. Probably because she hung around her father all the time, which isn't typical nine-year-old behavior in my experience. Since I spent most of my time in Vermont watching the only channel, I never saw that much of her.

Apart from her weirdness, it was true that Parsley and I looked alike. Not only brown hair but *springy* brown hair. And pale skin that never tanned, even in summer. And a pointy look around the chin and nose. We both took after my Aunt Lyle. What would she have said about the wedding, I wondered?

While I was imagining Aunt Lyle's comments, Nan-Ellen paced the room with a faint smile on her face. She was off in storyland. Aunt Lyle had never tuned out like that, as far as I can remember. But then Nan-Ellen isn't one bit like Aunt Lyle, or Parsley, or me. Not even physically. There's nothing pale or pointy-faced about her, for instance. Her hair is curly, not springy. She tries to keep it pinned up on her head but it never stays, and I have to admit that the more it straggles down, the nicer it looks. That evening it was a real mess and it looked fantastic. Come to think of it, that evening she looked about eighteen. Suddenly the truth dawned on me: My mother was in love. How could I have been so dumb as not to notice?

"Okay, so Uncle Jack is the Flaming Passion of Your Life," I said, making it sound like something in the soaps. "I still don't see why we have to live in Vermont. Why can't he and Parsley move down here?"

I shouldn't have asked. Nan-Ellen launched into a song and dance about how Uncle Jack couldn't move the company he worked for, but a writer could write anywhere. She reminded me that she was about to start her thirty-first book. I had heard a lot about her thirty-first book, because she kept saying that this one would get an award.

"—and of all the places to write, what could be

better than in the country, where it's quiet?"

"Want a list?"

"Of course, with so many cats around, I may not be able to type for sneezing," she continued, ignoring me.

That caught my attention. We had spent Thanksgiving, Christmas, and a week each summer in Vermont since long before my parents got divorced. In that entire time, Uncle Jack had never let a cat into the house. He had a good reason.

"Cats?" I repeated. "How come he has cats all of a sudden? You're *allergic* to cats!"

Nan-Ellen shrugged. "They're strays that Parsley's brought home. Lots of them, it seems. Jack has told her they have to go, but apparently she can't find any of their owners."

"Weird!" I said.

Nan-Ellen nodded. "Jack says it's hard to believe they were abandoned. That might make sense in September, he says, because summer people have been known to leave their pets behind when they go back to the city. But it's only July, and it seems like almost every day Parsley brings home another. Jack has been asking around, but he says—"

I was getting tired of what Uncle Jack said. "Who cares what he says? The point is, that's one more reason not to move in with him. Those cats could kill you! People die every day of allergies; I heard that on TV. It's no joke."

"Don't exaggerate," Nan-Ellen said. "I thought you'd be glad to hear about the cats. You're the one who's been begging for a pet all your life. Now that we're moving to the country, you can have one."

"One of Parsley's stray cats? Thanks a bunch!"

"How about a dog?" she said temptingly. "Or gerbils, or whatever. You name it."

"You mean I could have a canary?"

She hesitated before answering, "Why not?"

This may sound dumb, but when I was a little kid, I wanted a canary. Not a dog or a gerbil, just a canary. Once I actually did save up my allowance, and brought a canary home from Woolworth's, but Nan-Ellen made me take it back again. She has this thing about pets not belonging in the city, and birds not belonging in cages anywhere. If she was hoping to bribe me now by giving in about the canary, she had a big surprise coming: I was twelve years old, and unbribable. Instead of jumping with joy, I turned on the TV again and switched from channel to channel. Ordinarily, this is a sure bet for getting Nan-Ellen out of my bedroom. She kept right on talking, though. Most of the talk was about Uncle Jack and his house up in Vermont.

"Just imagine, a month from now you'll be there!" she said dreamily. "No more ugly high-rise buildings when you look out your bedroom window, just fields and trees. Pine trees, and birches, and maples—and at night you'll see every star in the heavens. Won't that be wonderful?"

"I like *this* view."

"It'll be wonderful," she continued, not hearing my answer. "We'll be close to nature, close to the earth. We'll bake our own bread and eat home-grown vegetables."

"Whose home-grown vegetables?" I asked. "Uncle Jack buys his, just like us."

"Not from the same place, though," Nan-Ellen corrected me. "The supermarket vegetables he buys aren't organically grown like the ones we get from the health-food store. After you and I move in, things are going to change."

I told her to quit dreaming. I reminded her that Uncle Jack had a full-time job, and she'd be too busy writing her new book. She just laughed.

"Just think—you'll pull your own carrots out of the ground! You'll pick your apples off the tree! You'll reach under the hen for the egg you eat for breakfast!"

"What hen?" I asked.

"Your hen. You can start from scratch with eggs in an incubator. Then all these cute little yellow chicks will hatch. Won't that be an improvement on life in a Boston high rise?"

11

Looking back, I realize I should have congratulated her about the wedding. Plus I should have felt relieved and happy. Someone else would be in charge, after all. I could forget my dad's parting instructions and start leading my own life. That's not quite how it went, though. The way it went was, I got mad.

"No!" I shouted. "No, it certainly will not! I'd hate it, and so would you. If you think I'll let you do a crazy thing like that, you've got another think coming."

Nan-Ellen's face turned pink, which is a sure sign of trouble. Narrowing her eyes, she gave me a long, hard look. "Let me?"

"I promised Dad!" I said. Then I chickened out and added, "Oh, never mind."

"Don't give me 'never mind'—it's too late to back down now! What do you mean, you 'promised Dad'? Did he tell you to take care of me? Do I strike you as the kind of woman who needs taking care of?"

My embarrassment only made things worse.

"You agree with him, don't you!" she said angrily. "The two of you have got *some nerve*. I'm earning a decent income, and I've raised a healthy kid. This means I'm incompetent?"

I let out a sigh of defeat and mumbled, "Sorry."

After a long silence, Nan-Ellen sighed too and put her arms around me. "I can take care of myself,

Owen. Even if I couldn't, which is an absurd idea, I'll have another adult to help me now."

I stiffened against the hug. "In other words, you don't need me anymore?"

"In other words, you can be a kid again," she said. "It's supposed to be fun being a kid, so relax and enjoy yourself. Okay?"

I was almost too mad to speak, but I couldn't get her to leave my room until I said I'd try.

Two

THERE WAS A POWER FAILURE the night we moved in with Uncle Jack. I was standing at the window of the room that from now on would be mine when all of a sudden everything went dark. And I mean really dark—like nothing I had ever seen back home in Boston.

I squinted to see if I could make out the outline of trees, or the shed, or Nan-Ellen's car. It was no use. I knew what was out there, but I couldn't see a thing.

On the other hand, there was plenty to hear and smell. The rain, for instance. The first drops stirred up the dust until my nostrils hurt. Once they got going, they rattled on the metal roof like a snaredrum roll. It had rained plenty of times before when I stayed with Uncle Jack, but then the house was bright and cozy. This total darkness made me homesick. When it rained in the city, the streets would get covered with a kind of slick, rainbow sheen that sprayed up each time a car drove by. Back home in Boston you could *see* the rain.

Besides which, even for August it was hot. Rain ought to bring coolness, especially at night. But this rain seemed to have rounded up all the heat in Vermont and driven it into my bedroom. I opened the window to let some of it out again, but it was stuffy outside, too. I tried not to think of that other window, back home in Boston.

Parsley was in the room next door. She kept bumping into things and saying "Jeesum!" which I guessed was the closest most Vermont kids get to swearing. I knew she wanted to make me feel sorry for her. I knew she hoped I'd call out and ask if she was okay. But I was caught in my homesick mood so I waited for her to call first.

"Owen?"

Another weird thing about Parsley is her voice. Mostly she speaks in a whisper. Sometimes, if she makes an effort, she can raise it to a squeak. I didn't answer until I heard the squeak.

"Owen Noonan!"

"What?"

15

"Where's Daddy?"

"Downstairs, I guess."

"Do you have a flashlight? I can't find mine."

"What do you need it for?"

"Jeesum, what do you think I need it for? To see, of course. Daddy called the power company, but they said it would be a couple of hours."

"City hours or country hours?" I called back.

"What's the difference?"

"A city hour means sixty minutes. Out in the sticks here, it could mean tomorrow morning."

Parsley appeared in my doorway. That is, I heard her appear. I still couldn't see a thing.

"Do you have a flashlight or don't you?" she asked. "I didn't hear."

"That's because I didn't say."

She waited. I tried to ignore her and concentrate on feeling homesick, but she made me so uncomfortable that after a few minutes I felt around in my duffel bag for the flashlight I had packed the day before, and turned it on.

"Here. But if you wear out the batteries, you have to replace them. With alkalines."

"Thanks, Owen!" Parsley swung the light around and shone it in my face, suddenly blinding me. "How come you're not using it yourself?"

Ordinarily I don't pick on little kids. Parsley was the only one around to pick on, though, and my

16

mood had gotten the better of me. "Use it? What for? Can you name one thing in this dump that's worth lighting up?"

"Yes!" Parsley answered in her weird, whispery voice.

She left the room without telling what that one thing was. Probably on purpose to annoy me.

"Okay, let's hear it!" I called after her. "What do you need that flashlight for?"

She didn't answer. I stumbled after her down the hallway until I found the door to her room, but it was locked.

"What have you got in there?" I asked. "Open up!"

She didn't open and she didn't answer.

"Come on, Parsley! Let me in."

I pressed my ear against the wooden door. It felt cool against my cheek. There wasn't a sound on the other side, not even breathing. I got down on my stomach on the floor and tried to look underneath. There was a half-inch crack: big enough to fit my fingers through. But no light showed at all.

"If you're not using my flashlight, I want it back!" I called. "I want to go downstairs, and I don't intend to break my neck getting there."

When she still didn't answer, I considered breaking in. It was while I was getting to my feet again that I felt a key in the lock. On the *outside* of the door. So how did she lock herself in—was there a hook on the other side? I couldn't resist. Slowly and quietly I turned the key, removed it, and slipped it into my pocket.

I know it wasn't the nicest thing in the world to do to someone, let alone a cousin who was about to become my kid sister. But it gave me a mean, powerful feeling that was an improvement on homesick. And I really intended to unlock that door again the minute Parsley complained. Only I forgot.

The reason I forgot was that I felt hungry. Wishing more than ever that I hadn't lent Parsley my flashlight, I groped my way downstairs to the kitchen, where I was relieved to see a hazy, golden glow.

"Nan-Ellen?" I called.

The answering voice was gruff, but friendly. "Your mother wandered off half an hour ago and never came back. I bet she thought it was the perfect time to begin her new book."

I laughed. "Trust her not to notice when the lights go off!"

"She notices more than she lets on," Uncle Jack told me reprovingly. "Don't let her fool you with that spacey act of hers."

He was making sandwiches by candlelight. Barefoot, wearing the faded red bathing trunks he jogs in when he gets home from work and a T-shirt he got for donating to Vermont Public Radio. The T-shirt had holes in it. I took a close look at him in case he had developed some new attraction. Not that he was so bad to begin with; I had nothing against him as an uncle. It's just that I couldn't see him as the man who would marry my mother. And he had no right to tell me I didn't know what she was like!

"Nan-Ellen could use a seeing-eye dog," I said to set him straight. "Like, this one time last spring she thought her electric typewriter was broken. She was already on the phone with the repairman when I told her she forgot to plug it in. I mean, she might have actually paid the guy to plug in her typewriter for her if I hadn't been there. Would you believe it?"

I thought he'd laugh, but his answer was "It could happen to anyone. Your mother is not a flake."

He said this sternly, but then he winked at me. That's typical of Uncle Jack; his face sort of contradicts itself. Meaning that his mouth is stubborn but his eyes send you friendly messages, as if they had a lot to say if his mouth would only let them say it. They twinkle at you from under his bushy eyebrows even if he happens to be scolding you. It was hard to tell whether he was scolding me that evening in the kitchen. One thing was sure: He thought he knew Nan-Ellen better than I did. I gave him the cold shoulder for a while, but he was too busy making sandwiches to notice.

Even by candlelight, there was something weird about those sandwiches. Looking more carefully, I noticed that they were made with hot-dog rolls. I don't mind hot-dog rolls when they have hot dogs in them, but these didn't. Uncle Jack was trying to spread cold peanut butter on them. He was making a real mess.

"Are those for Parsley?" I asked.

"Parsley and I had supper before you got here. But your mother said she was hungry after that long drive."

If Nan-Ellen was hungry, I knew it wouldn't be for processed peanut butter spread on hot-dog rolls. I poked at the package on the kitchen counter. "What happened; did you run out of bread?"

"Your mother said *she'd* provide the bread. I guess she forgot."

"She didn't forget," I corrected him. "She means now that we're real Vermonters, we're going to bake our own."

Uncle Jack gave me an uneasy look from under his bushy brows. "Who's 'we'?"

"When she says 'we,' it usually means me unless I can think up a good excuse," I explained. "Back home in Boston, I did a lot of our cooking."

Uncle Jack said all I needed was to keep plenty of dirt under my fingernails. Then he grinned at me. "When you walk into a kitchen with clean hands, you're just asking for trouble. I found that out when I was a kid myself. Moral: Don't wash your hands until you're ready to eat."

"I don't mind helping," I said. "I always make the sandwiches back home. The problem is, I don't think Nan-Ellen will eat this stuff. I do most of the shopping too, and she always says to get peanut butter at the health-food store."

Uncle Jack slapped an oily brown glob on a roll and began to smear it around. "This brand suits me and Parsley fine."

Somehow the conversation was going wrong. I stood there awkwardly, watching him arrange the mangled sandwiches on a plate. "Want me to give you a hand?" I asked after a while.

"I can handle it," he said. Then he added, "How about tracking down your mother and telling her supper is ready? You'll have to take a candle, though. She took my flashlight when she left."

The problem with candles is that each time you meet a draft, the flame goes out. It was slow going. I stubbed my toe twice, and whacked my elbow so hard against a doorknob that for revenge, I kicked the door. I happened to be barefoot, so that hurt too. As I stumbled along, I thought of things I wished I'd said to Uncle Jack.

For instance: "You don't know Nan-Ellen the way I do. There's a thing or two you might learn from me before you take over."

He would have laughed. To him, I was just a kid. He had no idea how dependent on me my mother was before she got the crazy idea of moving to Vermont.

"What she needs is someone steady," I muttered to myself as I searched the rooms on the second floor. "What she needs—"

"What *who* needs?" a voice demanded.

I jumped about a foot. In the light of the candle, I barely made out Nan-Ellen standing in the doorway of the screened-in sleeping porch.

"Just talking to myself," I said. "Uncle Jack says to tell you supper is ready. How come you're in the dark? I thought he gave you his flashlight."

"I've seen all I want to see. I was going to use this as a workroom, but who could write a book in the middle of this zoo?" She handed me the flashlight. Then she made a little gasping noise and sneezed.

I had been through this at least a dozen times. When Nan-Ellen is about to start another book, she fusses around looking for a new and original place to write it just like a mother cat looks for a new and original place to have her kittens. Except I guess that's an unkind comparison, considering how she practically keels over if she comes within a mile of a cat.

The sneeze made me suspicious, and so did the smell. The sleeping porch was usually a well-aired place, but not tonight. I switched on the flashlight and knew straight off what had produced that smell: The place was full of cages.

Nan-Ellen moaned. "Parsley's strays."

Stray cats? I moved closer to make sure, and she was right. Never in my life had I seen so many cats in such a small space! They were crowded into eight cages. Each cage had a file card thumbtacked to it with names printed in big block letters.

"Tom Kitten and Miss Moppet," I read aloud. "Jenny; Pickles the Fire Cat. If they're strays, how does she know their names? They're not wearing collars or anything."

"She probably named them herself," Nan-Ellen suggested. "Out of books, you know."

"What books? This one's Rotten Ralph. How did she ever think that up? Oh, and here's Garfield! Parsley chose a good name for him. He really *does* look like the one in the books."

This time it was Nan-Ellen's turn to ask, "What books?"

"All of them. Like for instance *Garfield Weighs In*."

Nan-Ellen said that was a comic strip, not a book. I told her to go look in my bedroom and see for herself: I owned twenty volumes of Garfield. If those weren't books, what were they?

"Comic strips," she said. "Will you listen to that rain? You'd think it would cool things down, but I'm about to suffocate."

"It's the cats that are making you feel that way," I said indignantly. "Uncle Jack must be crazy to let Parsley keep them in the house. He knows you're allergic."

"They're on the porch, not in the house," she corrected me.

"So? You're still suffocating, aren't you?"

"It's not just the cats," Nan-Ellen said. "It's this awful weather too."

I gave up. Moving the beam of light from cage to cage, I kept on reading. "The Three Little Kittens; Puss in Boots; Calico Cat. Hey, look at the expression on this one's face! Parsley named him The Cheshire Cat after the Walt Disney character!"

"Walt Disney? You mean Lewis Carroll, don't you?" Nan-Ellen sneezed five times in a row. The noise must have scared the cats, because some of them started yowling so loud that for a while I could no longer hear the rain cascading off the gutters.

"This one's name is Snowball," I continued. "He

looks kind of mean."

"He was mean to Margolo."

"To who?"

Nan-Ellen groaned. "I can't believe you've never read *Stuart Little*. Did you say supper was ready? I'd better get out of here while I can still breathe, and I'll need the flashlight to get downstairs."

"Just a second," I said, shining the beam at the last cage. "She named this one Picky-picky. Parsley has a really weird imagination!"

"Parsley and Beverly Cleary combined would be more like it." She pulled a wad of tissue out of her pocket and blew her nose. "Owen, please! I'm dying!"

On our way downstairs, I asked if Beverly was a friend of Parsley's. This made Nan-Ellen groan again, only louder this time.

"What's the problem?"

"Nothing new," she answered wearily. "I just keep wondering how I ended up with a nonreader for a son."

I must have heard her say that a million times already. I was getting tired of it, so this time I pointed out that she was responsible.

She stopped dead in her tracks. "Responsible for what?"

"For my TV," I said. "If you weren't a famous author, I never could have afforded it. You paid me a fortune for helping out at book signings, right? If you were an ordinary mother, I'd be getting an ordinary allowance and I'd have to read books like ordinary kids."

I had hoped this would get another laugh out of her, but I should have known better. She was devastated and actually threatened to confiscate my TV set.

"Uncle Jack only gets one channel," I reminded her quickly. "Up here in bake-your-own-bread land, there's no way I could be an addict."

Nan-Ellen sighed. "Okay. But all the same, I can't believe you've forgotten the Ramona books. I used to read them aloud to you. Remember books? White pages with little black marks on them?"

"Oh, yeah!" I said. "They had those back home in the city. Back in Boston, you could actually read them, too. Remember Boston? The place with electric lights?"

I had the final word in that discussion. All my mother got was the final sneeze.

Three

NAN-ELLEN WAS STILL SNEEZING when we reached the kitchen. "Cats!" she explained to Uncle Jack. "Why didn't you warn me they were up there?"

He made a remorseful face. "Sorry! I meant to move them before you came this afternoon, but what with the heat and all, it slipped my mind. If it gets one degree hotter, I'm going to melt!"

"Nan-Ellen feels that way too," I informed him. "Only it's worse for her because she can't breathe."

It was too dark to be sure, but I think Uncle Jack gave me a dirty look. "I get the point, Owen. I'll remind Parsley to move them out of there. Where *is* Parsley, by the way? Off reading somewhere by candlelight?"

"Flashlight," I said. "She borrowed mine."

"Whatever," he grumbled. "You can't believe how worried I've been about her. She used to spend a lot of time with me, but now all she does is go off by herself and read. She's been this way ever since school let out."

Obviously my mother wasn't going to complain about Parsley's reading. If anything, she would complain about Uncle Jack trying to stop her.

"Count your blessings!" she said indignantly. "Owen has no interest in the printed word unless it's in *TV Guide*. Besides, weren't you worried last summer because Parsley didn't read enough?"

"That was you," said Uncle Jack.

Nan-Ellen ignored him. "She can't be spending all her time reading if she collected—how many stray cats is it now?"

"Eleven," said Uncle Jack, but I corrected him.

"Fourteen, at the latest count. You must have left out the three cutsie little kittens. How come you let Parsley collect all those cats, anyway? Do you *want* Nan-Ellen to get sick?"

This time there was no doubt about the dirty look. "I've known your mother longer than you have, Owen. Believe me, I'm aware of her allergy."

"Well, pardon me!" I said. But I made sure my voice didn't sound as if I meant it.

Uncle Jack looked annoyed. I guessed he'd really light into me if Nan-Ellen weren't there. "I know the cats are a problem," he said carefully, keeping his voice level. "Don't worry; their days are numbered. I already told Parsley she has to get them out of there. So couldn't we just forget about them while we're having supper?"

Proudly clutching the plate of mangled sandwiches as if it were a Thanksgiving turkey, he led us to the dining room. Nan-Ellen followed with a candlestick in each hand. The table was already set. Not only were there place mats and the special china, there was also a Mason jar stuffed full of goldenrod. I wondered if Uncle Jack had gone out to pick it in the dark. The whole setup was a surprise to me; generally, we ate in the kitchen.

"We may as well pretend we're doing this on purpose," Uncle Jack explained. "You know: romantic candlelight dinner on the evening you move in."

He gave my mother an idiotic smile, so I asked, "Want me to leave you two lovebirds alone?"

Nan-Ellen said not to be silly. Judging by the way she smiled back at him, however, she wouldn't have noticed if I disappeared. She had this lovey-dovey expression on her face. When Uncle Jack passed the sandwiches, she took one without looking.

I held my breath as my health-food mother took

her first big bite. I let it out again in disgust when she said, "It's going to be nice having a husband who can cook!"

"Gourmet peanut butter on gourmet hot-dog rolls," I commented. They paid no attention to me.

Apart from the way Uncle Jack and my mother looked at each other, the conversation was far from romantic. In fact, what they talked about was me: what I'd have to do to register for junior high, and whether the health form from my old school would do for my new one. After they got that straight, they tried to figure out if my schedule would let me walk Parsley down to her school bus in the morning so Uncle Jack wouldn't have to do it anymore himself. Boring! I tuned out for a while and was well into my fourth sandwich before I tuned in again.

"What can Parsley be up to?" Nan-Ellen asked, glancing at the empty place. "She can't have been reading by flashlight all this time."

"I wouldn't put it past her," said Uncle Jack. "I wish I could get her to spend more time outdoors, the way she did last summer. Maybe she will, now that Owen is here."

Nan-Ellen looked doubtful. "It's more likely he'll convert her to television. Have you tried talking to her? She may have some kind of problem."

When I heard her say "problem," I nearly threw

up. Why did she always find other people's kids so interesting?

"If you want a problem, I've got one," I announced. "I've reached the point of spontaneous combustion. How come you didn't bring our air conditioner?"

"I never dreamed we'd need it in Vermont, so I sold it to the new tenant."

"Great!" I said. "Just great! Don't tell me why; let me guess. Now that we're real Vermonters, we can make our own, right?"

That was one of my better lines, but she didn't laugh. When I tried to think of something funnier, everything came out mean. Like, we could fold up the pages of her manuscript to make paper fans. Or maybe if we kept the fourteen cats, she could sneeze up a breeze. Better yet, I'd suggest that Uncle Jack could provide the air conditioning, since he thought he was so cool.

All of a sudden, lightning flashed across the sky. I started counting the seconds until the thunder. "One Mississippi, two Mississippi—"

Instead of thunder we heard a lot of thumps and bumps upstairs.

Nan-Ellen looked up. "What on earth?"

I felt a chill of guilt as I fumbled for the key in my pocket. "Whoops! I'm afraid that's Parsley."

Uncle Jack shook his head. "Can't be. Parsley

never makes loud noises. Sometimes I wish she would."

I grabbed the flashlight and ran upstairs before they could ask any questions. It wasn't easy fitting the key into the lock, because the batteries were getting low. By the time the door was finally open, I was all set to apologize. Instead, I gasped.

Parsley had been locked into a second-story bedroom. I knew for sure she couldn't have climbed out her window, but she was soaking wet. What's more, she was shivering with cold. So was the thing she held protectively against her chest. A wet, furry thing that wailed like a baby!

Parsley laughed. "Jeesum, Owen! Scared of cats?"

I shone the flashlight on her pale, pointy little face. Then I shone it on the cat. "Where did that thing come from? Don't tell me you had it in your room."

Parsley shook her head. "I rescued it."

"From what? A dump truck? It looks like something you'd want to throw away."

"From drowning, silly. Daddy won't let me keep it, though. Could we say it's yours?"

"No way," I said.

"Please, Owen? Pretty please?"

She twisted her face into a fake pathetic look that made me want to puke. I was about to remind her of my mother's allergy when we heard footsteps on the stairs.

"Is anything wrong?" Uncle Jack asked, aiming his flashlight at Parsley. When he saw the cat, he whispered, "Oh, my God!"

"What is it?" Nan-Ellen wanted to know. "How did Parsley get so wet?"

Parsley clutched the cat so tight that it let out a wail. "This is Tao. I'll only keep him for a while."

"Absolutely not!" said Uncle Jack.

Parsley fixed her pathetic eyes on him, but he shook his head. "Out of the question. I don't know where you found this one, but it goes straight back again."

"Please? I can't take it back. It was drowning in the river."

"Sorry, sweetheart." Uncle Jack's voice was gentle, but I could tell he meant business. "You've got fourteen of them to find homes for already."

"I'll keep it in my room," Parsley promised.

"You'll do nothing of the sort."

"In my room with the door shut. I swear!"

"Parsley—" Uncle Jack's voice took on a threatening tone.

Nan-Ellen interrupted. "Jack, honey, you can see for yourself the child is distressed. She ought to go take a bath and change her clothes. Does it have to be settled right now?"

"Yes," he said. "Why this sudden epidemic of stray cats? It just doesn't make sense! I wish she'd tell me where she really gets them."

"I do!" said Parsley. "I always tell you. It's your own fault if you don't believe me."

He gave her a reproachful glance. "In a river, you said? The closest river is ten miles from here."

"People don't realize how awful it is for a cat to swim," Parsley said defiantly. "They only do it if it's a matter of life and death. Bodger and Luath were going to leave poor Tao behind, so he jumped into the river and—"

I didn't see what was so funny about making up a big fat lie, but Nan-Ellen burst out laughing.

"She's been reading *The Incredible Journey*! But Tao doesn't drown, sweetie. He gets rescued by a little girl named Helvi."

Parsley looked relieved. "Really? I haven't read that far. All I know is he gets hit on the head by a log and Bodger can't see him anymore."

"Keep on reading," Nan-Ellen said. "He'll be okay in the end; you'll see."

It was obvious that the two of them had totally forgotten the point of the conversation. Not Uncle Jack, though. "She has to put that cat outside before she reads another page," he said firmly.

Parsley shot him a look of horror. "In the rain? He's sick, Daddy. He'll die of pneumonia!"

"Put him in the shed, then. Give him a bowl of milk if you like. Out there, not in the house. Now, let's stop talking about it."

"Let's not," I said. "Let's *not* stop talking about it!"

Nan-Ellen made a quick movement with her hands. "Owen! Can't you see she's upset?"

I didn't care. "She still hasn't said where it came from, or how she got so wet. Not outside, that's for sure. She was locked in her room!"

I should have known that would get me in trouble. Sure enough, Parsley went to work on Nan-Ellen with her big, pathetic eyes. "Owen locked me into my room," she whined. "I was scared when I got back. And my room was much too hot."

"When you got back from where?" I demanded. "If you were locked in, how did you get to wherever it was?"

Nan-Ellen frowned at me. "Stop making things worse, Owen. There's no need for air conditioners in Vermont, but tomorrow we could drive out to Sears and buy a couple of fans."

"I don't need a fan," Parsley said. "It was freezing down by that river! Tao should stay with me until he gets warm again."

Uncle Jack gripped Parsley firmly by the elbow and steered her toward the stairs. "That cat goes out to the shed, and I mean now. Tomorrow morning, you can move the rest out too. What if Nan-Ellen gets too sick to be at her own wedding on Saturday?"

I don't know whether it was the mention of sneezing that did it or not, but suddenly Nan-Ellen bent over double with her worst attack so far. She got up to nineteen sneezes before she stopped. Then she started gasping to catch her breath. She looked scared.

"Want me to get your medicine?" I asked.

She shook her head, still gasping for breath, and managed a reassuring smile. Not at me—at Uncle Jack, who had stopped in his tracks. He went back and put his arms around her for a while. Neither one of them noticed the expression on Parsley's face. I did, though, and it really freaked me out. It was triumphant.

→→ *Four* ←←

NAN-ELLEN AND I were silent until we heard the
screen door bang. Then we went down and cleaned
up the supper mess by candlelight while she told
me what she thought of my behavior.

"Even though we've all known each other forever,
we have to be extra caring just now because we're
settling into a new pattern," she explained, winding
up her lecture.

I told her to stop talking like a book.

"What am I supposed to talk like, a TV set? This
is no time for you to make things difficult."

"Me?" I protested. "Parsley's the one who's acting
weird."

Nan-Ellen told me to put myself in Parsley's shoes. "She's had your uncle to herself since your Aunt Lyle died, remember? Now she has to share. With time, she'll come to terms with the new situation."

That last sentence sounded familiar. After a rapid mental search, I remembered why: It came straight off one of Nan-Ellen's book flaps.

"We're talking about Parsley, not about that kid in *Daddy Dates a Demon*."

Nan-Ellen wriggled her shoulders impatiently. "Can't you see it's a similar situation?"

"Sure," I said. "Except the stepmother in that book was a child abuser, and you're not. Plus I'm in a similar situation too, right? I've had you to myself for over two years now, and I'm sharing, aren't I?"

"Are you?" Nan-Ellen asked.

"What do you mean? Of course I am!"

"Think about it."

If there's any more despicable, low-down phrase that grown-ups use, I've yet to hear it. No one has the right to tell other people what they should think about. It's patronizing. So I glared at her, and she glared back. It turned into a contest that lasted until the screen door slammed and we heard someone going back upstairs. I recognized Parsley's footsteps. I also recognized her voice. She was chanting a kind of rhyme, repeating the same lines over and over:

"Travel far,
Pay no fare,
Let a story
Take you there!"

"What a funny child!" Nan-Ellen said.

"Funny in the head, for sure," I agreed.

Nan-Ellen said, "Don't deceive yourself. She's as sane as you and I. She's just dealing with her father's remarriage by retreating into books."

As she listened to Parsley, the dreamy expression returned to her face. I knew what was coming. "Don't tell me," I said. "She's going to be the heroine of number thirty-one."

Nan-Ellen looked doubtful. "Number thirty was a girl, so I should make it a boy this time. I like to alternate, you know."

I knew. That was the whole point; I knew practically everything about Nan-Ellen, but it didn't seem to matter anymore. I began to feel sorry for myself. Uncle Jack mattered, and Parsley, but not me. I was expected to stay cool and not make trouble. Not act human, in other words. It really made me mad.

"Did you ever consider writing about a boy whose problem is that he doesn't have a problem?"

Nan-Ellen gave me a startled look. "What do you mean?"

"Like, at home he's just your average guy. And he's no trouble in school, so the teachers hardly notice him. Then maybe one day he disappears, and his mother doesn't even miss him until she runs out of granola. Because he was the one who used to shop for groceries. Get it?"

Nan-Ellen said she got it, but she didn't think she could use it. "It's too negative," she said. "It would be boring."

Boring!

"Well, how about this for an idea?" I continued, although it was hard to talk straight, I felt so mad. "How about a boy whose mother comes on strong while she's single, but neglects him once she finds a husband. Or is that boring too?"

I watched Nan-Ellen's face in the flickering candlelight while she gave it careful consideration. Was I going to get through to her this time?

Apparently not. Frowning thoughtfully, she answered, "It's been done."

That's where my last scrap of self-control abandoned me. "I'll say it's been done!" I shouted. "It's still being done, and you're the one who's doing it. Don't you care about anybody but yourself?"

Her mouth dropped open. It looked as if I was finally getting her attention! Only that's when my soon-to-be stepfather walked in.

"Parsley's gone to bed," he announced. "She was all wiped out." Then he noticed our faces and asked, "Is something wrong?"

"I guess that depends on how Parsley reacts to the latest news," I answered sarcastically. "This famous children's author is using her as a heroine."

Uncle Jack ignored the sarcasm. "She'll be thrilled! If I were you, though, I wouldn't tell her until tomorrow at breakfast."

"Whatever you say," I said in what I have to admit was a really nasty voice. "I wouldn't want to upset the little princess. Unlike the rest of us, she has to deal with this so-called situation, right?"

He was too baffled to answer, so I made a dramatic exit. Then I took his advice, except for the part about breakfast; I couldn't wait that long. The reason was, my TV had been on when the power went off, and I'd forgotten about it by the time I went to bed. It came on again at dawn, in the middle of the business report. I couldn't get back to sleep, so I woke up Parsley.

"My mother is putting you in her new book!" I announced as I walked into her room.

Parsley yawned and rubbed her eyes. When she got through rubbing them, she squinted at the clock on her bedside table. Then she glared at me.

"Jeesum, Owen! It's only five thirty-seven!"

"Sorry," I said. "But did you hear me?"

She shrugged. "I heard you. Big deal! I've been in lots of books."

Her answer was so unexpected that for a moment, I didn't know what to say. Then I repeated: "Lots of books?"

"Lots." Parsley stared at me without blinking her eyes, which are a slightly greener blue than mine.

"Name one!" I demanded.

The Incredible Journey," she said. "That's where I got the cat last night. And before you came yesterday, I went to Carabas and brought back Puss in Boots."

"To where?" I asked.

"To Carabas. At least, I think that's the name of the place. Remember the fairy tale?"

I shook my head, so she explained. "The cat pretends his master is the Marquis of Carabas, and he fools the ogre and makes it so his master gets the ogre's land and castle and all."

I studied her face. It was serious, but there was a glint of mischief all the same. "Get real!" I said. "Where did you *really* get those cats?"

"I already told you," she insisted crossly. "Out of books. Will you leave? I want to go back to sleep."

"Not until I get an honest answer."

Parsley flopped down in bed and hid her face in her pillow. If she thought this would make me leave, she was wrong! Humming to myself, I checked out her room. It was a normal one for a kid her age. Socks and underpants on the floor, for instance. I didn't look too closely. There were a few attempts at the ruffled look that some girls think they need for self-respect: flowered wallpaper, and the same pattern on a lampshade. And she had tacked posters on her wall, mostly of unicorns with rainbows in the background.

I was jealous. Not of the ruffles, but of the lived-in look. So far my room still felt like a guest room, even though it was the same one I used each time I came to stay. Would it ever become my own place, littered with my own clothes and posters and books?

Parsley had a lot of books. Most of them were on shelves or on her bedside table. One was lying in the middle of the floor with a green bookmark tucked between its pages. I picked it up and read the title aloud.

"*Alice's Adventures in Wonderland.* I saw a rerun of that on Channel Thirteen. You're going to like it."

Parsley lifted her head from the pillow. "If you're talking about the Disney movie, I hated it. All those gooey voices! The book is great, though. I went in to get the Cheshire Cat, and afterward I went to the Mad Hatter's tea party. I met Alice and the March Hare."

"Grow up," I said. Then I paused. "The March Hare is the one that looks like Bugs Bunny, right? I remember, he's cute."

"He is not!" Parsley protested. "In the book, he's

dreadful. Every bit as rude as the Mad Hatter, but not nearly as funny. The Dormouse was cute, though. I tried to hug him, but he bit my arm."

I said, "Yeah, sure!"

Parsley rolled up her pajama sleeve. There were two gross-looking scabs just above her scrawny elbow.

"That's a dormouse bite?" I asked.

She nodded. "It bled a lot until Alice tied it up with the Mad Hatter's bowtie."

I bit my lip to keep from laughing. "His bowtie, huh? That doesn't sound very hygienic to me. How come she didn't use a table napkin?"

Parsley looked shocked. "Are you kidding! Do you know how long that party had been going on? Months! It was summertime—July, maybe, because Alice is about to make a daisy chain before she goes down the rabbit hole—and the party started in March. Those napkins were disgusting!"

"Uh-huh."

"I think the March Hare spills a lot," she told me confidentially. "He seems kind of clumsy. While I was there, he spilled the milk jug into his plate. That's why he wanted to move to the next place over. They were always moving to the next place over at that party. But Alice had to mop up the milk with her napkin."

"Tell me about it."

"The bowtie made a pretty good bandage," she continued, taking me literally. "I had a terrible time getting the blood out afterward, though. I want to keep it as a souvenir."

I grinned in spite of myself. "A souvenir bowtie?"

"Why not? I've decided to collect things from all the books I visit from now on. There's nothing special about bowties, though, so today I'm going back in for something better."

Was the kid making fun of me? "It sounds like a dumb game," I said scornfully. "Want to come watch TV?"

Parsley shook her head and reached for a length of cloth that was draped over her bedside table. There was no doubt that it was a bowtie. It was the same shape as the one my dad wore with a rented tuxedo once, only this one was white with big red polka dots.

"Whose is it really?" I asked.

"It's the Mad Hatter's."

I groaned. "Stop trying to act cute and tell me the truth, why don't you?"

Parsley looked me straight in the eyes. "I can go inside books," she said. "You can too. Read what it says on that bookmark if you don't believe me."

I drew out the green bookmark and studied it carefully. "VERMONT SUMMER READING MARATHON" was printed on it in big block letters.

Underneath was a poem:

Travel far,

Pay no fare,

Let a story

Take you there!

On the back of the bookmark, there was a lot of small print explaining about the marathon, like how the prize went to the kid who read the most books, and how the program finished on August thirty-first.

"The thirty-first is the day after tomorrow," I said. "How many books have you read?"

"Only three, all the way through," said Parsley. "I'm not trying to win. It's more fun just going inside."

I took a deep breath and reminded myself that she was only nine years old. "Get real, Parsley! All that poem means is that you can go somewhere with your imagination. Not with your whole body."

Parsley shook her head impatiently. "But you can! That's what I keep telling you. The librarian gives out bookmarks to every kid in school for the summer marathon. Last year's bookmark didn't do what it said, but this one works just fine."

"What do you mean, last year's didn't do what it said? What does a bookmark have to do, besides keep your place in a book?"

Parsley sighed as if I were deliberately being stupid. "It ought to do what it promises. Otherwise it's dishonest. Last year's bookmark said 'Free Mileage: Books Can Take You Around the World!' But it didn't work."

"Surprise, surprise!"

She yawned again and smiled impishly at me. "Well, to tell the truth I didn't think it would either. But I tried this one on a Ramona book, and before I knew what was happening, I was in Ramona Quimby's kitchen. Luckily no one was there but Picky-picky. The Quimbys were all outdoors."

"Which explains how you brought the first cat home," I said. "Nice story, Parsley. Got any more good stories for the others?"

I should have learned by then that Parsley is immune to sarcasm. "I told you, they all came out of stories."

"Why just cats?" I asked, trying a different tactic. "Why not something more exciting, like unicorns?"

"Promise not to tell?"

"Sure," I said easily.

"Cross your heart and hope to die?"

"A slow and agonizing death." I was smiling by now—she really was a funny kid.

Parsley shot me a sly glance. "Is your mom allergic to unicorns?"

I started laughing when I got the point. Parsley didn't like the idea of the marriage any better than I did myself. We were in the same boat, with this difference: She didn't just complain, she took action. Her dad was about to marry a woman with an allergy to cats, so she brought in cats. Fifteen of them, to be exact. It was hilarious!

"How about Sylvester, and Tom from *Tom and Jerry*?" I suggested, practically peeing in my pants, I was laughing so hard. "Hey, and isn't there a cat in *The Smurfs*?"

"Those are just television cats," said Parsley. "I bet they wouldn't even make her sneeze. You heard what Daddy said last night, didn't you? I want her to be too sick to be at her own wedding. I want her to get sick enough so she goes back to Boston. Maybe she'll even die."

I stopped laughing. "Hey, wait a minute. That's my *mother* you're talking about. Besides, I thought you liked her!"

"She makes an okay aunt."

"Okay?" I repeated angrily. "Just okay? Do you realize how many kids all over the United States— all over the world, even—are crazy about Nan-Ellen Noonan?"

Parsley nodded. "I never said I didn't like her books."

"You have nothing against her; you just want her

dead, right? Did it ever occur to you that I might feel the same way about Uncle Jack?"

She looked at me solemnly. "If you agree with me, why don't you help out?"

"Help make my mother sick?" I asked. "You're even weirder than I thought if you expect me to do a thing like that. Uncle Jack is right to be worried about you, and I'm going to tell him so."

"But you promised!" Parsley wailed.

I left her room in a thundering rage, but her question stuck with me. I didn't want Nan-Ellen to get sick, of course. Last night's attack wasn't something I'd care to see again. But there was no danger of that, because from now on, she'd make sure to stay away from Parsley's cats. *Far* away. Maybe as far away as Boston. She could still marry Uncle Jack, if she really loved him. But he'd have to move in with us, not the other way around. It wasn't my idea of heaven, but I could handle it. And if filling the house with cats could bring it about, why not help Parsley?

"How about *The Aristocats*?" I said aloud.

Taking a deep breath, I forced myself back to reality. It was just a kid's game, not something that could really happen. Parsley might have found a clever way to make Nan-Ellen leave, but she sure as heck didn't do it by physically going into books. The question was, where *did* she get those cats?

➤➤ *Five* ◀◀

EARLY MORNING IS NOT my best time. It's creepy being awake when everyone else is asleep, and there's
nothing worth watching on TV. In Vermont, make
that less than nothing. I sat through the *Morning
News* and *The Flintstones* on channel 3. Then the
wind must have changed, because I couldn't get
channel 3 anymore, but channel 8 came in just
fine. Meaning I got to watch the weather. Big deal!
I already knew the weather: hot. After breakfast, I
planned to follow the stream downhill. If I was
lucky, I'd find a place where the storm had made it
deep enough to swim. Once I found it, I planned to
stay all day.

By the time I heard noises in the kitchen, I was starved. I could have gotten my own breakfast earlier, of course, but it would have been Cheerios and milk. I was hoping for something fancier. Uncle Jack usually made pancakes on the first morning of our visit, and served them with blueberries and local maple syrup. My mouth was already watering as I hurried downstairs.

"Run for shelter!" I yelled. "The pancake killer strikes again!"

But the kitchen was empty. A cereal bowl had been left on the counter with some flecks of granola floating soggily in the last spoonful of milk. One more tradition down the drain! I did some mental detective work. Parsley was still asleep, and Uncle Jack wasn't big on granola. It must have been my mother who had eaten in such a hurry. Did that mean she was driving into town? I ran to the window and looked out.

Uncle Jack's driveway is a dirt one, and it's narrow. There are maple trees on both sides. Their branches meet overhead, making a tunnel of speckled light and shadow. That morning about fifty puddles were steaming away out there, left over from the storm. Nan-Ellen's car was parked in the middle of the largest puddle. It wasn't going anywhere. The door of Uncle Jack's red pickup truck was open, though, and Uncle Jack was trying to climb inside with a coffee mug in one hand and his briefcase in the other. I watched while my mother took the mug, then handed it back through the window. Uncle Jack grabbed her wrist and held it until she stuck her head in to kiss him good-bye. It was a nauseating scene.

"I don't get the point of the pickup," I told Nan-Ellen when she came back inside. "He's an accountant, not a farmer. Is he trying to act macho or something?"

She blinked at me a few times. I noticed that her eyes were red; those cats were still getting to her. "I thought you loved riding in the pickup. What made you change your mind?"

In my experience, grown-ups answer questions with questions too often. It's a way of putting you in your place. However, two can play at that game.

"What happened to the pancake breakfast?" I asked. "Isn't that supposed to be a tradition?"

Nan-Ellen said that we could have Uncle Jack's pancakes anytime, because we were here to stay. "He was late for work this morning," she added. "He only had time for a bowl of granola."

I feigned astonishment. "Granola? My uncle Jack? You've got to be kidding! He's too macho for granola."

"He didn't use to like it," Nan-Ellen said, frowning. "Now he's giving it a try. We all have to look at this as a kind of readjustment period, Owen. Lots of our habits have sharp edges, right? We need to smooth them down a little so we fit together as a family."

"Remind me again why we need to be a family?"

By this time, I was asking the questions. Nan-Ellen was looking more and more defensive. That's psychology! I asked one more, just to show I had the upper hand.

"What happened to the cat last night? Did they really shut it up in the shed, or did they just let it go?"

Nan-Ellen said that Tao was in the shed, but by no means shut up. "We want him to go back where he belongs," she explained. "Parsley took out some scraps, though, so there's not much hope. Once you feed them—"

I felt torn in two directions. On the one hand, I was ready to go along with anything that inspired my mother to cancel the wedding and move back to the city. On the other, Parsley was a scheming little brat who got away with murder.

"Why feed the ones in the house, then?" I asked, following her back into the kitchen. "Why not let them loose in the shed so they can catch mice until they leave?"

"That's what your uncle said. His exact words, almost. You're two of a kind!"

I didn't appreciate the compliment, but it wasn't the moment to say so. "Why not, then?"

She sighed. "The problem is, Parsley is such a sensitive kid. High-strung. It's a big change, having us move in like this. I'd be happy to get those cats out, but I don't want to rock the boat."

"Parsley will survive."

Scrunching her face into a worried-mom look, she continued. "Jack is worried about her. He says she doesn't hang out with other kids enough. She's too attached to him, and she needs to transfer a lot of those feelings to someone nearer her own age. Like you, Owen."

"Hey, cool!" I said. "She can call me 'Daddy.' Then you can finally write a book about me, and call it *Confessions of a Preteen Father*."

Believe it or not, Nan-Ellen Noonan laughed. Progress! Taking advantage of what seemed a better mood, I asked if I could spend the day down at the stream. Her response was enthusiastic.

"What a great idea! Jack was just saying how Parsley doesn't spend enough time outside."

There was a congealed puddle of wax where a candle had been, on the kitchen counter. I picked at it. "I hadn't planned on taking Parsley."

But Nan-Ellen had tuned me out by then. She wasn't even looking at me. Instead, she was trying to figure out how to work the propane stove. She has been using it for years, but between visits she forgets.

"I'm going alone," I informed her. Louder, this time.

Nan-Ellen squinted at the stove, turned a few knobs, then chickened out and turned them off again.

"Mom!"

That got her attention. I only call her "Mom" about once a year. "What is it, Owen?"

"I may not have any say in who you marry, but I sure as heck get to decide what kids I sit for," I said firmly. "I'm not sitting for Parsley, so get that straight. The kid isn't normal."

She flashed me a mocking grin. "What makes you an authority on normal?"

Pancakes not being on the menu that morning, I was fixing myself a bowl of Cheerios after all. Nan-Ellen's attitude annoyed me so much that my hand shook, and I poured about half a cup of milk on the kitchen floor.

"Are you kidding? Normal is how most kids act. Me, for instance."

Nan-Ellen stopped grinning, but the mocking look stayed in her eyes. "I see. Normal is holding a grudge against everyone. Normal is assuming that if things don't work the way you want them to, it's somebody else's fault, not yours."

55

Taking a deep breath, she turned the knob for a back burner. After a moment of suspense there was a sickly smell, followed by a billow of blue flame. "I'll never get used to this!" she wailed.

"Thanks for listening," I said as I backed away from the stove. "Thanks for caring how I feel."

When she finally turned to look at me, her face was pale. "Have you any idea how *I* feel, Owen? Has it occurred to you that *my* happiness is at stake here too? Couldn't you bear with me until things settle down a little, the way Parsley does?"

"Parsley!"

"Yes, Parsley. She may have problems dealing with the situation, but at least she accepts it."

That was the final straw. "For your information, Parsley is so far from accepting the situation that she's thought up a plan to make you leave. Want to hear it?"

"No," said Nan-Ellen. "I want you to take her swimming."

That was her final word, so I left the room. What's the use of arguing? Grown-ups make up the rules in this world. Luckily it was the end of summer, not the beginning. In a few days, Parsley would be back in school.

"I'm going down to the stream," I told her. "You might as well come too."

Was Parsley grateful? Guess again. I practically

had to beg her to come! "I don't know if I should," she kept repeating primly. "Daddy wants us to move those cages."

"Forget the cages," I finally said. "If Nan-Ellen has an asthma attack, it's her own fault."

The idea of an asthma attack was so appealing to Parsley that she danced out of the house and was headed for the back field before I could stop her.

"Hey, where are you going?" I shouted. "That's not how you get to the stream!"

"It's a shortcut," she called back. "My way takes us straight down to where the water gets deep."

Parsley's way may have been shorter as the crow flies, but we weren't crows. A field lay between the house and the woods, and the sun nearly burned us to a crisp while we were crossing it. What's more, we had trouble even getting into the field because it was separated from the backyard by two barriers: an old stone wall, and some electric fencing wire. The neighbor's cows were in the field. That meant the current was on, so we had to get down on our bellies and slither under.

"I've gotten shocks a couple of times, and it's nothing," Parsley boasted. "I don't know why people are so scared of touching electric fences."

"If it's nothing, let's see you do it now," I dared her.

Parsley ignored me. "I wonder if there's a bull in

here. Are you scared of bulls too, Owen?"

"What do you mean by 'too'? I'm not afraid of electric fences; I'm just being practical."

"Practical," she repeated thoughtfully. "I was thinking of going into *The Story of Ferdinand* and bringing Ferdinand back to this field, but I decided it wasn't practical."

"Ferdinand the bull?" I asked. "I saw that on TV."

Parsley gave me a scornful glance. "I bet the book is better than the cartoon. Jeesum, it's lucky I'm the one who got the bookmark! On you it would be wasted."

"You're right," I said. "What would I do with it?"

"You could help me bring home some cats, that's what. It may take a few more to convince your mom to move out."

I didn't know whether to get mad or laugh. Was Parsley so anxious to get rid of me? She must know I had to go wherever Nan-Ellen went until I got a little older.

"You have to admit it's working!" she continued happily. "Have you noticed how feeble your mom looked this morning? I just wish I could find a book about a pet store, so I could bring back a whole bunch at once."

I laughed in spite of myself. "You're crazy, Parsley. No one ever got a cat out of a book."

"How do you know?"

"I know because it's impossible, that's how. If you could really take something out of a book, the next time you read the book it wouldn't be there anymore."

I thought that clinched the argument, but Parsley doesn't give up easily. "That's what I thought too," she agreed. "Like for instance, I was holding Picky-picky when the bookmark brought me home from the Ramona book. So I started reading ahead to see what the Quimbys would do when they found out he was gone. Only he wasn't. He came in at all the right places for the whole rest of the book. It didn't even say I'd been to visit."

"That proves my point," I said.

Parsley said no, it proved hers. Swinging her backpack to the ground, she stopped to rest. The pack was heavy because she had jammed it full of stuff: towels, drinks, and sandwiches. Even a book! What's the point of going swimming if you get hot again lugging your backpack home? I hadn't brought anything, not even a sandwich, so no way was I going to help her carry it.

All the same, I waited while she caught her breath. Waited and sweated. The heat in that open field was so fierce that it made my ears hum. I thought things would get better once we reached the pine woods, but the lower branches were dead and spiky, and a pain to push through. Parsley's shortcut was longer than the road. In fact, I was convinced we were lost until I heard the stream.

With a sudden spurt of energy, Parsley darted ahead. "Last one in is a rotten egg!"

I had guessed right. After the rain, the stream was deep enough to swim in. The water was browner than usual; it must have flooded the banks upstream. Still, I figured it was good, clean dirt. Parsley stripped off her jeans but kept her T-shirt over a faded bathing suit. When she dunked in the stream, the shirt billowed out like a parachute. She lay back, making lazy ripples with her finger.

"This is the life!" I cried, following her in. "Hey, you forgot to take your watch off!"

Parsley let her breath out and sank to the bottom. Then she sat bolt upright, gasping for breath. Brown trickles of water streaked her face.

"Your watch," I repeated. "I sure hope it's water-proof."

"Of course it is," said Parsley. "It also tells the date, including what year it is."

"So what's new?" I asked.

"*That's* new, for the Mad Hatter. He'd never heard of a watch that tells what year it is. I promised I'd bring it back and show it to him. Thanks for re-minding me!"

She splashed out of the water and hurried to-ward her backpack. Draping a towel around her shoulders, she grabbed a sandwich with one hand and her book with the other. Then she waded across to a high, dry rock in the middle of the stream.

"I'm going to read," she announced. "You can have a sandwich if you like. Even though you didn't help carry my pack."

I held off for a while out of pride, but I got hungrier by the minute, watching her eat. At last I gave in. "How about if I carry it home?"

Parsley grinned and turned a page. "There's salami, or there's P-B-and-J. Be my guest!"

By that time I was ravenous, so I made a mad dash for the backpack. And it was only a few yards away. My point is, it couldn't have taken me more than a few seconds to get there. Plus another few seconds to reach in for the sandwich. At the very most, not more than ten seconds in all. But when I turned around, Parsley was gone.

⇢⇢ Six ⇠⇠

AT FIRST I THOUGHT IT WAS some stupid hide-and-seek. Little kids like to hide. Mostly they hide in obvious places because they think you can't see them if they can't see you. So I looked behind the rock that her book was still lying on, and behind a tree or two.

"I wonder where Parsley is," I kept saying in the kind of voice grown-ups use when they play peekaboo with babies. "Is she over here? Nope. Is she over there? Where could she be?"

I felt like a fool, but I told myself it wouldn't hurt to play for a while, considering how nice she'd been about the sandwich. For a while, not forever. It was too boring.

"Okay, I give up!" I called. "You win, kiddo. Come on out!"

There wasn't a sound—no crackling leaves, no snapping twigs, not even a giggle. It occurred to me that she might be peeing in the bushes. If so, I wasn't about to barge in on her. I sat down in the sun and waited. The heat felt good on my back after that cold swim, and it made me sleepy. I shut my eyes for what I meant to be only a moment. When I woke up, Parsley was still gone.

Had she left for home? Without her backpack? Without even taking her book? I waded out to the rock again and picked up *Alice's Adventures in Wonderland*. Parsley's place was marked with the green bookmark she had shown me that morning. "Let a story take you there!" Was that why she had jumped up from the stream? Did she really believe the bookmark would pick her up out of a hot day in August and set her down again in Wonderland?

It was a hardcover edition. The illustrations weren't by Disney—they were by a man named John Tenniel. I flipped through the pages, surprised at how different his drawings were from the Hollywood animation. Alice looked more interesting, for one thing. In the movie, she's sweet and innocent, but not too smart. The drawings made her seem sharper and kind of broody.

Parsley's bookmark was tucked into the middle

of a chapter called "A Mad Tea-Party." I returned to the beginning of the chapter and began to read. *"There was a table set out under a tree in front of the house, and the March Hare and the Hatter were having tea at it,"* it began.

As Nan-Ellen keeps reminding me, I'm not a reader. Which doesn't mean I can't decipher the words on a printed page—it just means I never really get involved to the point where I care what happens next. Result: I don't bother to turn the page. Not this time, though. Somehow I got caught up in the story. Why did the Hare and the Hatter tell Alice there was no room at the table? Why did they offer her wine when there wasn't any? It was totally wacky! Before I knew it, I had turned the page.

Then a weird thing happened. I didn't go anywhere, but I had the sense of traveling. For a moment I felt a little dizzy. I squeezed my eyes shut and waited for the feeling to go away. When I opened them and glanced down at the book again, there was no book. I was sitting at a table on someone's lawn, staring at a starched, white cloth. That is, the cloth had started out white. Now it was stained with tea and greasy smears of butter. Lots of places had been set, but most of them were empty. There was no sign of Parsley, but a blond girl sat in an overstuffed chair at the end. At her left was an enormous rabbit, next to him some other sort of animal, and then a man in a top hat. I caught my breath: It was just like the illustration. Those were the March Hare, the Dormouse, and the Mad Hatter—and the girl was Alice. I was dreaming about Wonderland!

Or was it a dream? Nothing I dreamed had ever felt so real. In dreams I don't smell, and this place smelled of freshly cut grass and burned toast. Plus something more unpleasant: stale tobacco mixed with sweat was my guess. I suspected the Hatter, who looked as if he hadn't changed his clothes for weeks.

Alice turned her head and stared, but she wasn't surprised to see me. In fact, her expression said that nothing would surprise her anymore. The others weren't surprised either. Just annoyed.

"It wasn't very civil of you to sit down without being invited," said the March Hare.

Ordinarily, I'd blush to invade someone's privacy, but this was absolutely not my fault. "It isn't your table, is it?" I asked. "I thought it was the Hatter's."

The Hatter looked down his big, hooked nose at the Hare and sneered. "Just what the other children said. The one in the armchair, and the one who promised she'd come back with her watch. They both said it wasn't your table, and they were both right."

"The one with the watch is my cousin Parsley," I said. "She ought to be here now. Haven't you seen her?"

"A skinny child?"

I nodded.

"Pale? Rather unhealthy looking? Green eyes?"

"That's Parsley," I agreed.

"Her hair wants cutting," said the Hatter.

"So what?" I said. "Have you seen her?"

The Hatter took a sip of tea and answered, "No."

"But you must have seen her if you can describe her like that," I said.

"Why?" he demanded.

"Because you couldn't describe her if you hadn't met her. Besides, you said she's coming back with her watch."

"Are you quite sure I've seen her?" the Hatter asked with a haughty glare.

"Of course you've seen her!"

"Then why ask?"

I groaned. "You're not making sense. The point is, she's lost. I don't know where she is."

"*You're* not making sense," said the Hare. "If you don't know where she is, you don't know that she's in the wrong place. And unless she's in the wrong place, she's not lost."

"That isn't what I meant," I murmured weakly.

"Then why say it?" snapped the Hare. "You are

uncivil, uninvited, and unkempt."

Alice had kept silent all this time, but I noticed some twitching around the corners of her mouth.

"I suppose you think it's funny!" I said angrily.

"If you don't laugh at them, they'll drive you mad," she warned me. "They're already quite mad themselves, so it's no use trying to reason. They talk in riddles."

The Hatter looked pleased. Rising slightly from his chair he asked, "Why is a raven like a writing-desk?"

I looked at Alice, but she shrugged. "He asked me that before, but I couldn't guess. I don't believe he knows the answer himself."

"It can't be too hard," I said. "All you have to do is think what they have in common. Let's see—you write with ink, and ravens are black as ink."

She shook her head politely.

"Well, then, how about this: You write with pens, and in olden times, they used feather pens. Ravens have feathers, so—"

"Wrong again!" said the Hatter. "One more chance."

I thought harder. "Is it something to do with bills?"

As far as I could tell, the Dormouse had been fast asleep since my arrival. He must have been listening, though, because he leaped from his chair and began to scamper around the table. "Fun, fun, fun!" he squealed. "It's all been so tediously dull, but now we'll have some fun!"

"Is he okay?" I asked Alice.

"Quite mad, like the rest of them," she assured me.

Giggling hysterically, the Dormouse scampered faster. "First guess wrong! Second guess wronger still! Third guess wrongest of all! Fun, fun, fun! Off with his head!"

"Excellent idea, what?" the Hatter muttered, leering at the Hare.

Off with my head? Wasn't there someone at the end of the movie who said that? A nasty, fat woman with beefy arms. That's right: the Queen of Hearts. "Off with her head!" she kept shouting at Alice. I remembered an executioner's ax, and a bunch of playing-card people running around with red and black spears while the music grew wilder and wilder. Then Alice woke up, because it was just a dream. What if I ended in a court of justice, sentenced to death by the Queen—would I wake up too?

"You're crazy!" I told the Dormouse. "You don't behead people just because they can't guess riddles."

"Behead, be dead! Behead, be dead!" shrieked the Dormouse. "Long live the Queen!"

"Why save him for the Queen?" asked the Hare. "Why not bite his head off now?"

I tried to convince myself that I shouldn't feel afraid. Suppose this was no dream? Suppose Parsley had been telling the truth about the bookmark taking me inside stories? According to her, it would bring me home again. This was just a story, and these were made-up characters. What was it that Alice had said at the end of the movie? "You're only a pack of cards!"

The problem was, these characters weren't cards, and they didn't look made-up. After all, isn't real what you see and feel? Their world was real now, not mine. The Dormouse had bitten Parsley. The March Hare had teeth too. Long yellow ones, streaked with brown. As for the Hatter, he had taken bites out of teacups in the movie. What was to keep him from taking bites out of me? It's no use telling yourself it's just a story when you're right in the middle of things. This was no TV show where I could turn down the sound or go to the kitchen for a soda.

Where was Parsley? She got me into this mess, so why didn't she get me out of it? Maybe she would turn up if I waited. I should keep them talking—try to buy time.

"It's my turn to ask *you* a riddle," I told the Hatter.

"It's nothing of the sort," he said, leaning across the table until his nose bumped my cheek.

I nearly threw up; he had terrible breath.

"Fair is fair," I said, although I suspected that this might not hold in Wonderland. "Why did the chicken cross the road? No, wait a minute—that's too easy. What's black and white and red all over?"

The Hatter smiled triumphantly and began to speak.

"Hold it!" I cried. "Forget that one—everybody knows it. Let me think a minute."

To my surprise, Alice beckoned to me. "No use playing fair," she whispered in my ear. "*He* won't. Ask him a riddle that has no answer."

So I took a deep breath and asked, "Why is a Mad Hare like a March Hatter?"

I swear I didn't say it that way on purpose. The last thing I needed was to offend them—it's just I was rattled, and not really thinking. But boy, were they ever offended! The Hare revealed another inch of yellow teeth, while the Hatter rose to his full height and stalked menacingly around the table toward the place where I was sitting.

"Stop!" I shouted. "I apologize!"

"Jeesum, Owen!" said a voice behind me. "What's your problem?"

Of all the times for my cousin to show up—cool as a cucumber and asking what's my problem!

70

"This maniac wants to kill me for not guessing the answer to a riddle, that's all," I told her breathlessly. "Where have you been?"

"Chatting with Frog Footman," said Parsley. "If the Hatter has already asked you the riddle, it's time to go home—I put the bookmark on that page."

Calmly stretching out her arm, she showed her wristwatch to the Hatter. He didn't look at it, though. With an evil gleam in his eye, he continued to advance toward me.

"Help!" I yelled.

There was a sudden scuffle. Just as the Hatter reached me, someone tackled him. Not Parsley—someone blond with long hair. It was Alice.

The Hatter fell. When I turned to run, I bumped into Parsley and we both fell too. The Hatter had no trouble getting away from Alice. He rose and stumbled toward us with a murderous expression on his face. It was too late to escape. Throwing my arms around Parsley, I shut my eyes.

"This is going to hurt," I thought in the last split second before he attacked. "This is going to be painful and bloody, and Nan-Ellen will never know where I went."

But nothing happened. The split second turned into half a minute, and the only sound was gently rippling water. Cautiously, I opened my eyes and found myself back at the stream.

Parsley was trembling, but she wore a smug expression on her face. "You can let go of me now."

I let go, feeling slightly ashamed of myself.

"Well?" she asked, splashing water on a scratch. "Now do you think I'm crazy?"

⤜ Seven ⤛

IT'S FUNNY HOW BEING SCARED can make you cold. For a while, I thought I'd never get warm again. Only a very short while, though. The day had grown hotter in Vermont, and by the time we got back to the house, I caught myself missing the climate in Wonderland.

"Is everyone in that book as weird as the Mad Hatter?" I asked Parsley.

"Want to go into a different chapter and find out?"

"No, thanks," I said. "That was enough for one day."

It was stifling inside the house, so we moved to the porch swing, where we sat with a pitcher of lemonade wedged between us. I poured myself a glass and brooded over our narrow escape from the tea party.

"Do you have any idea how much trouble that bookmark could get you into?" I asked Parsley.

Her lack of concern alarmed me, and a scary thought came into my head. "Did you say the librarian gave one like it to every kid in your class?"

Parsley nodded. "I think mine's the only one that works, though. Otherwise we would have heard about it."

"But why you?"

She shrugged. "I was just lucky, I guess."

I felt a pang of jealousy. Then I remembered that Nan-Ellen had put me in charge of her for the next few days. Didn't that put me in charge of the bookmark too?

"I'll say you were lucky!" I agreed. "You were lucky you were just reading some dumb kid's book the first time it happened. Otherwise you might have been gone forever."

"It seemed like forever," Parsley admitted. "I had to spend the weekend in the Ramona book, and I got homesick. I hate sleeping in other people's houses! I liked Ramona, though. I wish I could invite her to spend the weekend *here*."

I found that hard to swallow. "Come on! Your father would have been worried out of his mind. He would have called the police. What did you say when you showed up again: 'Sorry, guys, but I got stuck in a book'?"

Parsley laughed. "Of course not. You're only gone for as long as it would take to read that much. Half an hour, maybe. But the next time I was really careful how much time went by in the story."

It was a while before I got it straight. Apparently the bookmark served as a sort of escape hatch. After deciding how much of a story you wanted to visit, you put the bookmark next to the page where you wanted to come out. Then you went back and started reading. Everything you read came to life, and when you got to the marked page, you were home again. It didn't matter whether months or minutes went by in the story; you were away from home only the time it took to read that far.

"And you're sure nothing changes in the story afterward?" I asked.

She frowned thoughtfully. "Nothing changes in the book, at least."

"What's the difference?"

"Well, I'm visiting the story, see? The characters usually know I'm there, so that's a change for them. But I always read the book again when I get home, and it never changes, no matter what I do or how long I stay. I can prove it, if you like."

I took a long swig of lemonade. "Okay, prove it."

Alice's Adventures in Wonderland had been lying

on the floor. Parsley picked it up and flipped through the pages impatiently. "Read this aloud!" she commanded, pointing at the bottom of page 92.

Instead of the place where I went in, she had chosen the part a little farther on in the same chapter, where Alice looks at the Mad Hatter's watch. I began to read: *"'What a funny watch!' she remarked. 'It tells the day of the month, and doesn't tell what o'clock it is.'*

"'Why should it?' muttered the Hatter. 'Does your watch tell you what year it is?'"

Reaching into her jeans pocket, Parsley fished out something round at the end of a gold chain. It was an old-fashioned pocket watch I'd never seen before. Still, it didn't prove a thing.

"Give me a break!" I said. "You bought that at a flea market."

"Take a closer look," she advised me.

I had to admit it was weird. The hands pointed to one word, Wednesday.

"If it's the real thing, then you're a thief," I told her sternly. "How did you get it, anyway?"

"I grabbed it just before we left," said Parsley. "And you can't call me a thief, because it's still there on page ninety-two."

"That's not the point," I argued. "The point is, I won't have you using that bookmark for stealing other people's stuff. And I want to be really careful about choosing where we go from now on."

"*You?*" She gave me an outraged look. "It's my bookmark, isn't it? I get to choose where we go. And if you're mean to me, you can't come."

I could tell she meant what she said, so I shut up about the watch. "Where do you want to go next?"

"I can't decide: There's a cat called Dragon in *Mrs. Frisby and the Rats of NIMH*, or we could get Harry out of *The Cricket in Times Square*."

"Is Harry a cat?" I asked. "You've brought back enough cats already. And by the way, shouldn't we move them to the shed before Uncle Jack gets home?"

Parsley shrugged. "Yes, but let's not bother."

I couldn't believe it. "Wait a minute! That's why you didn't want to go swimming!"

"So I changed my mind," she said defiantly. "Your mom won't let Daddy get mad at me."

"Why not?"

"Because I'm sensitive, and she doesn't want to rock the boat." Parsley narrowed her eyes slyly before adding, "You thought I was still asleep, didn't you! And the whole time, I was on the other side of the door."

When I told her it was nothing to be proud of, she just laughed. It wasn't the first time I'd noticed that Parsley had no respect for other people's privacy.

"If you don't want any more cats, let's get some

things for my souvenir collection," she said. "I'd like one of those carved ivory elephants from Colin's house in *The Secret Garden*."

"That's stealing!" I objected. "Anyway, I saw that movie on TV, and it's terrible. Especially the soppy part at the end where Mary grows up and marries Colin when he's a soldier."

A horrified look passed over Parsley's face. Then she made a sputtering noise in her throat and laughed for about five minutes.

"What's so funny?"

"You!" she said. "You just made that up."

I shook my head. "I swear I didn't. It was on *Hallmark Hall of Fame*."

"Read the book," Parsley advised me. "Nobody grows up. Nobody gets married. You'll love it."

Parsley had brought a whole stack of books out to the porch with her, and *The Secret Garden* was one of them. I leafed through it quickly.

"There's an awful lot of small print," I said. "Besides, it looks like a girl's book."

She reminded me that there were two boys in it: one who starts out nice, and one who doesn't get nice until later. "You'd like it better than the movie," she said.

I had my doubts; it looked awfully long.

"I wouldn't mind having some water from the spring of eternal life in *Tuck Everlasting*," she said thoughtfully.

I didn't know the book, but the idea of Parsley being forever nine years old was a little scary. "What else do you have?" I asked.

She picked up a paperback with a picture of a mouse paddling a canoe on the cover. "I've already been into *Stuart Little* to get Snowball. It was fun! I was thinking I could go back again and bring back that cute little birchbark canoe."

"You can get one of those in any souvenir shop," I said scornfully. "Besides, I told you I'm not interested in stealing. Isn't there someplace exciting we could go?"

She thought for a moment before suggesting *Charlotte's Web*. "There's a fair with a Ferris wheel, and bumper cars. All kinds of rides. We might need money, though."

When I said, "I saw that story on TV," she groaned. "I bet you did. And I bet you thought it was cute. Did you think *Little Women* was cute too?"

I told her I'd never heard of it, so she reached down to her pile and handed me the heaviest book of all.

"Better read it," she said. "We're going inside."

My heart sank. A nine-year-old was reading this? It was nearly seven hundred pages long, and in spite of the illustrations, it looked tedious. Maybe *because* of the illustrations. They were mostly of girls in long dresses. They had faces like dolls' and stood in silly, doll-like poses.

I made a barfing noise. "No way!"

Parsley said I should give it a chance. "This takes place more than a hundred years ago, but Amy goes to Paris, France!" she said excitedly. "The only foreign place I've been is Montreal. We could go with her."

I made the mistake of asking who Amy was, so Parsley insisted on reading aloud from a chapter called "Experiments." I still don't know why she chose it, since nobody goes anywhere in it. In fact, that's the whole point: It's about four sisters who decide to take a week's vacation in their own home. I can think of a million fun things I'd do if Nan-Ellen gave me a week off from helping her, but all these girls did was lounge around. Like most old-fashioned books, it had a moral: They forgot to feed the canary and he died.

"*'Put him in the oven, and maybe he will get warm and revive,' said Amy hopefully,*" Parsley read. To my horror, she giggled.

"You've got to be kidding!" I said. "That's not funny, that's gross!"

Parsley looked up from the book in surprise. "You don't understand. Amy wants to put the bird in the oven like you'd put a turkey in the oven at Thanksgiving. Get it?"

I told her she was wrong. Amy wanted to bring

Pip back to life, not eat him. Even if she was right, it wasn't funny. "Show me that part," I said.

Parsley handed the book over and I read the passage again to myself. A sick feeling settled in a kind of lump, somewhere between my stomach and my throat.

"How about we go in and rescue him?"

"What for?" Parsley asked. "You wouldn't change anything. When we got home and read that part again, he'd die anyway."

I told her it was really unfair for Pip to have to die for a bunch of nerds like the March sisters. But instead of seeing it my way, Parsley got all defensive.

"You can't say they're nerds until you've read the whole book. It's wonderful! Even in the sad parts, like when Beth dies, it's wonderful."

I slammed the book shut and stared at it gloomily. "So she dies, does she? Well, she deserved it for killing her canary. I had a canary once. For one day. The next day, Nan-Ellen made me take it back to the store."

"What for?"

"She thinks birds aren't happy in cages. She's probably right. But that canary was going to be in somebody's cage, so why not mine? Now that we've moved to the country, she says I can have a canary again. As if I cared!"

"But you do, don't you?"

"Not as much as I did then. I don't even care that much about this one—it's just that killing him off makes it such a dumb story. What kind of dumb author would want to write about killing someone's pet?"

"Your mom would," said Parsley. "There's that part in *I Never Asked for Asthma* where the poodle gets mutilated by the lawn mower and has to be put to sleep. That story isn't dumb, it's great!"

I shook my head. "The story is okay, but the part about the poodle is dumb. It would have been a perfectly good book without it."

"It would have been a perfectly *boring* book," Parsley stated with conviction. A scheming expression spread across her face. "Remember the girl named Emily? She had a fourteen-karat-gold friendship ring. I'm going into *I Never Asked for Asthma* and getting that ring."

"You're not going to steal!" I shouted. "If you don't hand over that bookmark, I'm telling my mother on you!"

Parsley was too quick for me. Jumping down from the porch swing, she banged through the screen door and up the stairs. To her bedroom, I guessed. To spend the rest of the day stealing things for her collection. But it would be the last time, if I had anything to do with it.

⤖ *Eight* ⤖

MY MOTHER IS NOT ALWAYS the easiest person to find. Even back in our Boston apartment, she had a way of vanishing. That morning she had said she planned to get cracking on her new book, so I figured she was in the house. But there wasn't a sign of Nan-Ellen Noonan at work: no typewriter, no manuscript, not so much as a newly sharpened pencil. I finally found her outside in the vegetable garden. That is, in what used to be a garden. Right now it was a patch of weeds fenced on three sides by chicken wire, and on the fourth by the shed where Uncle Jack wanted us to move the cats.

"Hi, sweetie!" Nan-Ellen said. "What are you up to?"

I was still smoldering. "Have you got a minute? I need to talk to you about Parsley."

"That's nice," she said.

"What are *you* up to?" I asked. "I thought you were going to write all day."

Nan-Ellen said she'd come out for a breath of air. The cats were really getting to her, she explained. She wheezed a little, as if to prove her point. Then she pointed at the weeds. "Jack says he hasn't planted vegetables since your Aunt Lyle died, but those lumpy things look like squash to me."

"That's nice," I said sarcastically. I hate squash.

She smiled in agreement. "It must have seeded itself, and will you look how much there is? Enough to feed a family for a year!"

I looked and felt sick. "There were some needy families in my school, back in Boston. Maybe we could ship it down."

There are times when my mother is totally humorless. Ignoring my comment, she explained in gory detail how she would peel and steam the squash before packing it into jars. "I forget what you do after that, but I'll find out," she concluded.

"That's when you call UPS," I said. "What happened to your new book? There are millions of kids out there waiting for the next Nan-Ellen Noonan. To say nothing of your publishers."

Nan-Ellen said the publishers would have to

wait. She explained how they were city people who tended to forget that Nature has deadlines of her own. Then she asked me to tell Parsley to come out and help pick squash.

"Dream on!" I said. "Nobody tells Parsley to do anything. She's the stubbornest kid I ever met. Uncle Jack spoils her. You want to know what she's up to right now?"

I finally had her attention. "What *is* she doing right now? I thought you were going to keep an eye on her."

Here was my chance. "You'll never guess—" I began.

At the last minute, something made me hesitate. I wanted my mother's sympathy, but did I really want her to know about the bookmark?

"Out with it, Owen."

"Holed up somewhere with a book called *Little Women*," I said lamely.

Nan-Ellen smiled. "I loved that book too, when I was her age. I must have wept buckets over the part where Beth dies. What a tearjerker!"

When I told her that in my opinion Beth had it coming to her for starving the canary, a gleam of interest came into her eyes. "Does this mean that Parsley is teaching you to read?"

"I learned to read in first grade," I reminded her. "How insulting can you get?"

"Honey, I didn't mean you never learned to read," she said earnestly. "I just meant you don't seem to know how to enjoy it!"

I could feel my voice rising before I even said a word. "You've got some nerve! Who do you think you are, telling me I should enjoy reading! Do I go around telling you to enjoy TV?"

I gave her the coolest of my cool looks as I walked away, but inside I was in a boiling rage. I was glad I had kept quiet about the bookmark. If Parsley got in trouble, it would serve Nan-Ellen right. All the same, what if she really went inside *I Never Asked for Asthma*? What if she was caught stealing Emily's gold ring and got arrested or something? Would I be responsible? I ran up to her bedroom, taking the stairs two at a time. If she had locked herself in again, I'd break down that door!

As it turned out, I didn't even have to open it. Just as I skidded to a stop outside her room, Parsley walked out. She was holding something. Something small and yellow, cupped gently in her hands.

"This is for you, Owen," she said softly. "I know you said you didn't care anymore, but I thought it would make you feel better about the one you had to take back to the store."

I caught my breath. "Pip?"

She nodded. "Promise you won't read that chapter again, though. It would just make you feel sad."

I hardly heard her words. What did I care about *Little Women*? I finally had a pet of my own, and since we lived in the country, Nan-Ellen would let me keep it.

"Thanks!" I said.

It's funny how you can be mad at someone one moment and want to hug them the next. It's happened a million times with my mother, of course, but I never thought it would happen with a brat like Parsley. I forgave her a lot of stuff, right then and there. After all, I told myself, she was just a kid.

Giving her a big smile, I repeated, "Thanks. Thanks a lot!"

I reached for Pip, but Parsley drew back. "Just one minute, Owen Noonan. First you've got to say it's not stealing."

What could I do? When you take something that doesn't belong to you, it's stealing. But I wanted that canary, and a little voice in my head began to persuade me otherwise. Pip came from a story, not from real life. Tell a judge that you stole a bird out of a book and he'd say, "What are you, crazy?"

"Maybe you have a point there," I admitted.

She shook her head. "Not maybe; I do. So say it."

I gave in. "Okay. It's not stealing."

It hadn't occurred to Parsley to bring the cage back too, so we put Pip in an aquarium with a piece of wire screening on top to keep him from flying away. He didn't seem to mind. Then I took him to my room. As I said before, my room still looked like a guest room. All I had unpacked so far were my Garfield books and my TV. Moving the TV down to the floor, I set the aquarium in its place. As soon as I could, I'd find Pip a real bird cage. He already looked happy. In fact, he began to sing.

Uncle Jack was the first to notice. Looking up from the supper table that evening, he asked, "Is your television making that twittering sound, Owen? Go turn it off. We're making an effort not to waste power."

Even if it had been my TV, he could have come up with a friendlier way of mentioning it. I could tell from Nan-Ellen's reproachful look that she thought so too.

"He *does* make an effort," she said defensively. "When has he ever left it on before?"

"He leaves the light on every time he's been in the bathroom," said Uncle Jack.

Nan-Ellen's face turned pink: as usual, a warning sign. Not that it wasn't already fairly pink. She'd been out in the sun too long, plus she looked as if she had a cold. "I thought we were talking about television."

In Uncle Jack's place, I would have dropped the subject. Instead, he said that what they were really talking about was discipline. Referring to me, I gathered. When Nan-Ellen told him she could discipline her own son, I knew it was time to interrupt.

"For your information, that noise was made by a canary."

"I assume you're joking," said Uncle Jack. "The last thing we need is another stray in the house. Which reminds me: Have you moved those cats out to the shed yet?"

Without the slightest embarrassment, Parsley answered, "No."

If you ask me, she enjoyed the fight and hoped to prolong it for a while. Hadn't she overheard Nan-Ellen say that we shouldn't rock the boat? So when Uncle Jack hassled her about the cats, Parsley began to cry. Not actual tears, mind you; just teary sounds. Naturally, Nan-Ellen sprang to her defense.

"Jack, I thought I asked you to leave her alone about those cats! If I can live with them, you can too."

"You can't live with them. Look at your eyes! Besides, it's not the cats," he grumbled. "It's the principle of the thing. When I tell Parsley to do something, I expect her to do it."

"But in this case, aren't you being a little insensitive?"

Uncle Jack said she should give him credit for knowing how to raise his own daughter. It didn't seem such a terrible thing to say, but Nan-Ellen looked as if he had slapped her face. After that we all just kind of stared down into our plates. Which happened to be empty.

"What's for supper?" I asked, trying to lighten the atmosphere.

Supper was spaghetti, with something my mother presented as "Mystery Sauce." After serving Nan-Ellen, Uncle Jack caught up a clump of spaghetti with the tongs and dropped it on Parsley's plate. "Sauce?"

Parsley took one look and shook her head.

"What about you, Owen? Sauce?"

I said I'd have a little. On the side of the plate, though. Not on the spaghetti.

"What kind is it, anyway?" Uncle Jack helped himself, but instead of digging in, he poked at it doubtfully.

I could hardly blame him. Spaghetti sauce is supposed to be red, unless you go in for the gourmet creamy kind. This was a glutinous yellow, with flecks of green.

"It's made with the squash in your garden," Nan-Ellen said proudly. "You said you hadn't planted anything, so it's lucky I found it. What kind of squash is it? I had a terrible time peeling it!"

Uncle Jack put down his fork and blinked at her. "I didn't plant vegetables, is what I said. I planted gourds. Are you trying to tell me you cooked my gourds? They're for decoration, not for eating. Any fool knows that!"

This time it was Nan-Ellen's turn to get all teary. Uncle Jack apologized for calling her a fool and told her that the gourds didn't matter. He looked kind of annoyed though, so I could tell they did. Parsley laughed, which made things worse.

"Did you remember to sign me up for junior high?" I asked, to change the subject.

Uncle Jack said he had registered me that morning. "They want you to fill in a new health form, by the way. And you're supposed to hand in four book reports when school starts next Tuesday. Think you can manage that?"

Suddenly I wasn't hungry anymore. "Are you kidding? That's only five days from now! I'll have to use the ones I wrote last year."

And wouldn't you know it? That triggered an argument about whether it was honest to use my sixth-grade book reports a second time. An argument between Uncle Jack and Nan-Ellen, at least. Parsley and I had the sense to slip away.

⇛*Nine*⇚

"*YOU* SURE WERE NO HELP!" I said angrily.

Parsley gave me a cool stare. "Who wants to help? We want them to break up, don't we?"

I didn't like the way she put it. "Break up isn't what I had in mind. I meant, just not get married."

"Same difference," said Parsley.

But she was wrong. My mother and Uncle Jack probably couldn't just not get married; it wasn't a casual friendship anymore. If Nan-Ellen canceled the wedding, she would move out, taking me with her. Just me, not Pip.

I looked at Pip hopping around his aquarium and said, "The problem is, we gave up the lease on our apartment. Someone else lives there now."

Parsley was trying to interest Pip in a strand on spaghetti that she had saved for him. "So where will you live when you go back?"

"Who knows?" I said gloomily. "What I'm thinking is, maybe we should let up on our parents a bit. If they break up, I don't want them saying it was our fault."

Parsley's voice rose in panic. "But the wedding is on Saturday. That's the day after tomorrow!"

"I hardly have any time for those book reports," I said, changing the subject. "What am I going to do if I can't use the ones from last year?"

It's funny how easily Parsley can be distracted by the mention of books. "Don't worry about the reports," she said confidently. "You don't need to read those books, you know. We can just go there. Then you can write about what you see."

I told her I wasn't too fond of writing, either.

"I'll help you," she offered. "Want to do a report on *I Never Asked for Asthma*?"

"Forget it!" I said. "I already did one in sixth grade. Besides, you only want to go in for that ring. What I'd like is to go inside a story about animals. And I don't mean mutilated poodles."

Parsley thought for a moment. "Well, there's always *The Yearling*."

For once, I'd heard of it. "They made a movie of

that book! I've never watched it, but I saw it in the video store."

"You're not going to see a movie," Parsley reminded me. "You're going to see the real thing, but you'd better come to my room so I can tell you about it first."

It took her a while to find *The Yearling*. Once she had found it, she sat cross-legged on the floor with the book on her lap. I stretched out on the rug beside her, staring up at the ceiling while she told me about Jody Baxter. He lived in Florida, she explained. Not the vacation part of Florida with beaches and condominiums, but inland where there's just dry scrub, or else swamps. She told about Jody's loneliness, and how he had always wanted a pet.

"Like you, Owen!" she added. "Except it wasn't because they lived in the city that he couldn't have one; it was because his parents were too poor to spare the food."

She went on to describe how Jody finds this fawn, and his parents let him keep it. Her eyes grew huge and soft when she talked about Flag. She spoke eagerly, her voice rising and falling. She never doubted for a moment I'd be interested. She was right.

"The problem is, Flag keeps getting into the corn, and they need it for their cow and their old horse,

Caesar. So Pa Baxter tells Jody that he has to shoot the yearling. Then Jody says how he wouldn't mind being parted from Flag if only he knew that somewhere in the world he was still alive. Oh, Owen—it's so sad and beautiful!"

"Let's go right now," I said.

"I'll take you to the part just after Pa Baxter makes Jody take Flag out with his gun. It'll be March in Florida. After that we can go back to the year before, when Flag was born."

Parsley placed her bookmark carefully next to the page where she wanted to come home. Then she flipped back to the beginning of the chapter. *"Jody wandered west with Flag beside him—"* she read aloud.

I had the same dizzy, confused feeling as when I went into Wonderland, so it was a while before I could really take in the change of scene. When I did, the first thing I noticed was how different it felt to breathe. The air was humid, and thick with the smell of flowers. Looking around, I saw branches that were fat with blossoms. The ground where Parsley and I sat was covered with loose sand. Over our heads, pine trees were silhouetted against the sky. Scrawny Florida pines. Not a bit like the fat spruces that grew back in Vermont.

Just ahead of us, a blond-haired boy was walk-

95

ing. I guessed he was about my age. He was slim—even kind of scrawny, like those pines. He carried a shotgun over his shoulder. At his side, keeping pace with him, was a deer. It was a peaceful scene: just the two of them moving slowly through the fragrant spring air.

"Maybe we should have gone in somewhere else," I whispered. "This is too—too private."

"Shhh!" said Parsley. "Here's where he talks."

A moment later, Jody stopped and said aloud, "They cain't make me do it."

I remembered how Parsley had told me Jody was supposed to shoot Flag himself, and something tightened in my throat. I mean, this was no character in a book! This was a real kid who had always wanted a pet, and had finally got one, and now was going to lose it again in the most horrible imaginable way.

I must have made some sort of sound, because Parsley frowned and motioned for me to shut up. Making as little noise as possible, we followed until Jody reached a clearing. A tree with fragile clusters of lavender blossoms stood at the edge of it. Under the tree was a bed of soft green grass.

"There's the chinaberry tree that's in the story!" Parsley whispered. "Now he's going to lie down under it and cry."

Feelings I had never felt before rose up inside

me, swelling my chest so painfully that I wanted to rip them out and throw them away. It no longer felt wrong to spy on Jody, because his grief became my own. All I cared about was fixing things so he wouldn't lie down and cry.

"They can't make him do it!" I echoed.

I had spoken softly, but not softly enough. Flag cocked his head and stared at us with a frozen expression of alarm. Jody saw us too, and scowled so fiercely that his eyes narrowed into glinting blue slits.

"What are you doin' here? Git away!"

"We've come to help," I said, an idea forming in my mind.

Parsley turned a worried gaze on me. "We can't help him, Owen. You know we can't. No matter what we do, it won't change the book."

I didn't believe that anymore. If we took Flag back to Vermont, he would be gone from here, wouldn't he?

"We've come to help," I repeated stubbornly. "We're going to take Flag to a place where he won't get shot."

Parsley groaned. "Jeesum! What's Daddy going to say?"

Was she made of ice, I wondered? How could she look at the misery in Jody's face and not want to help him out? Then I looked at *her* face and knew that she agreed with me.

"We can save Flag," I told Jody. "Listen, do you remember when you said you wouldn't mind leaving him as long as you knew that he was alive somewhere in the world?"

Jody looked scared. "I never said that, I just thought it. How do you know what I was thinkin'?"

I couldn't say I'd read it in a book, so I quickly changed the subject. "We're from Vermont. We live on a farm up there, but we don't grow corn or anything, so Flag won't get in trouble. He can live with us. That's what you want, isn't it? Your mother won't shoot him after all."

I didn't expect Jody to act happy. All the same, I was unprepared for the horrified expression on his face. It wasn't because we were from Vermont, I realized. It was because it had never occurred to him, even in his worst nightmares, that his own mother would shoot Flag.

"Ma?" he said in a choked-up voice. "My ma?"

He turned so pale that his freckles stood out like cinders on snow. Tears welled up in his eyes.

"Don't!" I said quickly. "I know you're going to feel bad anyway with Flag gone, but at least he won't be dead. He'll live in the woods near our house. We'll put up notices that say no one can hunt there, I promise!"

Jody put his arms around Flag's neck and held

the yearling's head close to his own chest as if to protect him.

"No!" he said. "My ma wouldn't shoot nobody and you ain't takin' Flag noplace!"

I thought of Parsley's bookmark, stuck between two pages of *The Yearling* in her bedroom in Vermont. It was like a time bomb ticking away. What if it took us home without Flag?

"Don't you understand?" I asked, my voice rising in panic. "If we don't take Flag, he'll die!"

Jody's eyes widened with fear and doubt. His eyes flickered from me to Parsley and back to me again. "You mean if you take him, he'll live forever?"

I was about to promise that Flag would live forever, but I couldn't get the words out. Instead I said, "He'll die someday. But it'll be from old age, if I have anything to do with it."

There was a long, tense silence while we waited for Jody to decide. At last his face relaxed a little, and his arms went limp. Letting go of Flag, he backed away.

You could tell that Flag knew something was going on. I was afraid he would bolt—maybe run back to the Baxter farm. But he stood still, wide-eyed and wary. I put my arms around his neck the way Jody had and felt the muscles rippling under his skin. His neck was warm. The warmth spread into my body too, and made me feel happy all over. I looked up to smile at Jody, to tell him once more that Flag would be all right. But Flag and I were back in Parsley's room.

"You can wipe that grin off your face," Parsley told me. "We're in big trouble now!"

"Who cares?" I said. "He's safe with us. I bet this time the book changed."

Parsley shook her head. "Don't kid yourself. It never did before. It won't this time, either. Read the chapter, if you don't believe me."

I picked up the book, but I didn't open it. "You mean Flag dies anyway?"

Parsley reached for her hairbrush and began to groom the yearling with long, loving strokes. "Who cares?"

"I do," I said.

"Well, I do too, dummy. But I care about this Flag, not Flag in the book. We rescued this one and he's safe with us. That's all that matters, isn't it?"

I wasn't sure. "But if the book hasn't changed, we could go back and rescue another one," I reasoned. "If the book never changes, couldn't we keep on bringing yearlings home forever?"

"I don't know," Parsley said. "Anyway, what would we do with them all?"

Her question reminded me of a more urgent problem. "What are we going to do with this one?"

It was growing dark. Uncle Jack and Nan-Ellen were both inside, and likely to stay there until morning. It would be hard to smuggle Flag out without their noticing.

"Maybe they wouldn't mind," I said. "If we're letting him go anyway, they can't get too upset."

I saw by the look on Parsley's face that she didn't want to let Flag go. I didn't either.

"He used to sleep on Jody's bed," she said. "Tonight he'll sleep on mine. Then tomorrow, when no one's around, we can move him to the shed. There's plenty of room in there, if we move the lawn mower out of the way."

"He'll sleep on *my* bed," I said firmly. "It was my idea to bring him home."

"But it's my bookmark!" Parsley's words came snapping back at me like a tight rubber band. "Without it, Flag wouldn't be here at all. And if I can't have Flag on my bed, I won't let you use it anymore."

"Oh, yeah?" I tucked *The Yearling* under my arm. "We'll see about that."

Deftly, Parsley snatched her bookmark from between the pages and slipped it into her pocket. Then she turned her back on me and continued brushing Flag. "You're wonderful!" she crooned. "You're adorable! Oh, you sweet, cute, furry thing!"

There was no way I could win without making a

lot of noise, so I went back to my room.

It's funny the way people talk about how they feel mad. I guess what they mean is the tightness in their throat. I get that too, but when I'm mad, I mostly hear it. My ears whine and buzz. Sometimes they even throb. It doesn't hurt exactly, but it makes cool-headed thinking just about impossible.

As I lay on my bed, the whining and buzzing drowned out the sound of the new fan Uncle Jack had bought for my window. "It's not fair," I thought angrily. "Flag wouldn't be here now if it weren't for me."

What if I just grabbed Flag, and brought him back to my room? Wasn't I bigger than Parsley? And a whole lot stronger, too?

I knew the answer, of course. Flag would make a racket. Parsley and I would end up fighting. Our parents would hear, and nothing would be gained. What had we gained anyway, so far? If Parsley was right about nothing changing in the book, all we had done was create a new Flag rather than rescue the one that got shot.

Opening *The Yearling* to chapter 32, I began to read. She *was* right. Jody still threw himself on the grass under a chinaberry tree and cried. His mother still shot Flag in the leg. Jody still had to finish him off. There was nothing to show that Parsley and I had been there. After a few pages, my ears began to throb. I knew I should stop reading, but I couldn't put down the book.

"Flag is safe in Parsley's room," I kept telling myself. "The real Flag is here with us."

I didn't convince myself. When I got to the part where Flag is already wounded and looks up at Jody with his big, sad eyes, the book seemed realer than real life. So I lay down on my bed the way Jody lay down under the chinaberry tree. And like Jody, I cried.

⇢Ten⇠

I WAS STILL CRYING when Parsley walked in.

"Flag peed on my rug," she announced. "What should I do?"

"That's your problem," I said. "You wanted him in your room, remember? And knock next time, okay?"

My face was turned toward the wall, but I knew she was moving closer. "What's the matter?" she asked.

"Nothing."

She sat down on my bed. "What did you do, read that chapter again?"

I didn't answer.

Parsley was silent for a while. I could practically

hear her thinking. "It's not such a great idea to read those sad parts after you get home again," she said at last.

"I couldn't help it," I mumbled into my pillow. "I had to see if the book had changed."

Her voice became reproachful. "I warned you it wouldn't. But you shouldn't feel so bad about it. I told you, it's the story that counts, not the book."

"Aren't stories and books the same thing?"

Parsley was surprised at my question. "Of course not! A book is just a way to *remember* a story, like a photograph is a way to remember a friend."

I sat up and listened, willing to be convinced.

"When people change, old pictures of them don't change along with them," she continued. "If you cut your hair, for instance, it doesn't suddenly look short in every picture anyone ever took of you. It's the same with books."

"The same how?"

"The story is alive, see?" Parsley explained. "But the words an author writes down to tell it are sort of like photographs. No matter how much you and I change a *story*, the book will stay the same."

I knew that if I tried hard enough I might find some holes in Parsley's logic. I decided not to try, though. It hurt less to believe her.

One little question kept on nagging at me, all the same. "What if we took Flag back? Would there be two Flags then? And would both of them die in the book?"

Parsley rolled her eyes. "How should I know? The problem right now is, we have to get this one out of here. I bet he won't like going downstairs."

"I kind of guessed that," I said.

"Horses do it in movies, though," she added thoughtfully. "Maybe we could teach Flag."

I've seen a lot more movies than Parsley has. After reviewing them in my head for a moment, I said, "Those horses mostly go upstairs, not down. Upstairs might be easier."

I meant it as a joke, but she took me seriously. "That's brilliant, Owen! Let's take Flag to the attic right now, before the grown-ups go to bed. There's bound to be some time tomorrow when they're both out, and we can move him to the shed."

Brilliant? It was crazy! But once Parsley had it in her head, there was no stopping her. I didn't even want to after I had seen her bedroom. There were now two stains on the rug, plus a pile of droppings. The room smelled like a zoo, and Flag seemed to be hyperventilating.

"He's thirsty," I said.

"Me too," said Parsley, "but I'm potty-trained. Let's not give him a drink until he's on the kind of floor we can mop."

What we called the attic was a little room at the

top of the house that doubled as another guest bedroom. It had a cot that was always neatly made up with the sheet turned over an old patchwork quilt. But there was also a lot of interesting stuff, like Uncle Jack's army uniform, and old-fashioned appliances with frayed wires that would electrocute you in a flash if you were fool enough to plug them in. A bookshelf along one wall was crammed full of nothing but old *National Geographic*s. Other summers, when there was nothing good on TV, I used to go up and browse through them.

"It's hot up here," I said. "Are you sure Flag will be okay?"

Parsley opened the window to let in the night air. "He's used to the heat in Florida. We can stay awhile to make sure, if you like."

It was worse than Boston in a heat wave, but I figured if Flag could stand it, I could too. I helped Parsley roll up the rag rug and put it in a corner. We spread out some newspapers and brought up a bowl of water. Then we settled down to wait. I settled down, that is. On the cot, under the open window. But I guess Parsley doesn't feel the heat so much, being skinny like she is. She poked around the room restlessly, fiddling with the flaps of a toaster that looked like some kind of metallic beetle, and even trying on Uncle Jack's army jacket.

"Are you trying to get heatstroke or something?"

I asked. "Come look at this!"

I held up my favorite issue of *National Geographic*. It was dated July 1973 and had a picture of an erupting volcano on the cover. I must have looked at that issue dozens of times, but Parsley had never seen it.

"There's this article called 'A Village Fights for Its Life'," I told her. "It's about a volcano in Iceland called Kirkjufell."

I know that magazines and books aren't quite the same thing. Still, I got a kick out of having read something Parsley hadn't even heard of. She was fascinated, especially when she noticed that the men in the pictures were wearing coats.

"I thought volcanos only happened in hot places!" she said.

"Iceland is way up north," I informed her. "Besides, it says it's January, in the article."

"Vermont is way up north too. Do you suppose a volcano could erupt here in January?" Parsley didn't sound too happy about the idea.

I told her they could erupt anywhere, even in August. I happen to know this isn't true; some places just don't have the right type of geography. But it was kind of fun scaring her. "There was this man in Mexico who was plowing his field one day," I went on, making my voice low and spooky. "A volcano popped up right under his plow. I saw a documentary about it on TV."

Parsley shivered. "There wouldn't be room for a volcano in our field."

"A volcano could make room."

By this time she was completely freaked out, so I stopped teasing and read her the article instead. It starts on the deck of a ship. The author tells what the sky looks like, and that kind of stuff. Then the ship pulls up to a pier at an island called Heimaey, and there's a lot more description. No human beings get hurt. The only bad part is where an Icelandic pony runs into a stream of lava. It gets burned and blinded, so someone has to shoot it. Every time I read that part, I felt sick from imagining how scary it was for the pony. I skipped it this time, but Parsley was looking over my shoulder and noticed anyway.

"Poor pony!" she moaned. "The author doesn't even sound sorry for him. He's worse than Ma Baxter."

"It wasn't the author who shot him," I said. "It says here it was some fireman. He did it out of kindness. But otherwise, it says there were no casualties. I wish I'd been there. Volcanos are awesome!"

An idea popped into my head: such a fantastic idea that my heart started beating like crazy. "Hey, Parsley! Want to see some fireworks?"

She shook her head. "No way. It's too dangerous."

"We'll stay clear of the crater," I promised. "Where's that bookmark?"

I had a hard time persuading her. First I had to show her the part where it says nobody got hurt, and remind her how cool it was in Iceland, and things like that. The only reason she gave in was because of lava bombs. According to the article, these are lumps of solidified lava that get shot out by the volcano. Wouldn't you know it: Parsley wanted one for her collection.

"But I'm not going to stay long," she warned me.

I meant to choose the place where we went in, but Parsley was too quick for me. Wedging the bookmark between two pages of the article, she read aloud: *"We felt its hail of cinders long before we saw the volcano's fire—"*

A spray of icy rain lashed at our faces. The cot heaved, causing me to fall clumsily against Parsley. Except that it wasn't a cot any longer. It was the deck of a ship.

"You idiot!" I cried. "Couldn't you have waited until we found something warm to wear?"

Parsley fumbled with the buttons of her father's army jacket. "This *is* warm."

"Don't worry about me, okay?" I said bitterly. "I mean, what's a little frostbite?"

August seemed a million years away. So did Vermont with its peaceful night sky. Here the sky glowed orange in the distance as if an entire city were on fire. There was a rumbling sound. In Vermont it would have meant thunder, but here it meant something more deadly. Rain was not the only thing that fell on the deck; ashes fell, too. All of a sudden, I was scared. What had I gotten us into? This was no children's book. In fact, it wasn't a book at all. Maybe the bookmark worked differently with magazines. Parsley and I might be killed by molten lava, or trapped in the past forever.

Parsley grabbed my arm. "I changed my mind!" she wailed. "I want to go home!"

She knew as well as I did that we couldn't go home until we reached the part where she had put the bookmark. Meanwhile, we had some explaining to do. Voices shouted at us in a language that I didn't understand. Then a man moved toward us. He wore a blue turtleneck sweater under an open duffel coat, and he had a beard. He seemed more worried than angry, and to my relief he spoke English.

"Where did you two come from?" he asked.

Parsley just looked at him with big round eyes, so I said, "Vermont."

The man smiled the way people do when a little kid says something dumb, but cute. "What I meant was, what are you doing on this boat? Did you stow away? Are there any adults with you?"

I shook my head. Which was hanging down a little by now, I have to admit. Why hadn't it occurred to me that we would be trespassing?

"This is not a safe place for small children," he explained in a voice that sounded as if he thought we were both babies.

That's when Parsley found her tongue. "I'm only nine, but Owen is twelve," she said indignantly.

The man's smile began to look a little strained. "This is not Disneyland. It's for real. People could lose their lives."

"Don't worry, no one gets killed," Parsley reassured him. "Only a pony, when a fireman shoots him."

I gave her a dirty look. "Shut up!" I whispered. "You'll only make things worse."

"It was your idea," she reminded me.

The bearded man heard her and stopped smiling.

During this conversation, a group of men had gathered around us. One of them spoke lengthily in the language I didn't understand.

"This is the captain," the bearded man explained. "He says to tell you no one will harm you, but we need to know where your parents are so we can send a message to them. They're probably worried as hell. Did you think of that?"

"They're not worried," Parsley answered sweetly.

"We're not even born yet!" Fortunately, no one heard her.

But what if the man *could* send a message to the future? I wondered. I got this sudden mental picture of Nan-Ellen picking gourds on a hot day in Vermont and hearing the phone ring. She answers and someone says her son is on a boat in Iceland, heading for a volcanic island in the winter of 1973. If by some miracle she believed it, what could she do?

I imagined her calling the police. "Nan-Ellen Noonan here," she says. "Sorry to bother you, but my son seems to be lost in a magazine."

There's nothing she could do. We'd stay lost forever, in another time. We'd survive, of course. Someone would find us foster homes, and we'd grow up. We might eventually find our way back to Vermont. But it would be in someone else's time, not ours.

⇒⇒ *Eleven* ⇐⇐

THE BEARDED MAN INTERRUPTED my fantasy. "Didn't you hear me, kid? What's your name?"

Parsley answered for me. "His name is Owen Noonan. His mom is Nan-Ellen Noonan, the famous writer. She's my aunt and I'm his cousin. Except if we don't act fast, I'll end up being his sister."

The man let out a low, frustrated moan. He was losing his patience, but I didn't see what I could do about it. Would he be any happier if I said we'd used a magic bookmark to travel into an article that hadn't even been written yet? Then he'd lose his temper too.

I tried hard to think of something that would make things better, but I was too cold and scared.

"I'm sorry," I said, finally. "I guess this was a bad idea."

He just stood there for a while, shaking his head from side to side the way teachers do to show they're giving up on you. "We're pulling into the harbor," he told us. "Maybe someone there can help check this out."

One of the sailors handed me a jacket. It stank of fish, but I put it on gratefully and turned up the collar, because my ears felt like they were about to fall off. My fingers did, too. I worked each hand up inside the sleeve of the other arm and hugged my arms to my chest, trying to stop shivering.

"This is no fun," Parsley stated.

She was right, but it sure was spectacular. The volcano made a noise like thunder, guns, and fireworks combined. There was a constant glow over the peak. From time to time, these gorgeous sprays of fire shot into the air. I realized that what looked like a tongue of flame licking over the side of the cone was actually molten lava. It was all just like the article, only scarier. To me, the most impressive thing was the volcanic ash. As we pulled into the harbor, I could see it all over the place. It covered the streets. Some of the cars were half buried in it. And it was still falling.

If those ashes kept on falling, would we be buried too? I'd seen a TV show about ancient Pompeii where that had happened. I tried not to imagine breathing the ashes. Choking. Or running into the lava and getting burned and blinded like the pony.

"There were no casualties," I reminded myself. But those were just printed words, out of an old article. In no way did they make me feel safe. After all, the Mad Hatter attacked us when we went to Wonderland, even though there was nothing about it in the book. Something worse might happen to us here.

Parsley tugged at my sleeve. "Let's just stay on the boat. Okay, Owen?"

I agreed, relieved that it was her idea. So we settled down to watch the fireworks until the bookmark took us home. Or at least that was our intention. The bearded man ran off as soon as we had docked, but soon he came running back again.

"You're in luck!" he announced breathlessly. "There's a helicopter leaving for Keflavíc in a few minutes. The pilot says he's got room for you both, if you hurry."

Keflavíc? That was on the mainland, I remembered from the article. Miles away! Would the bookmark find us there?

Parsley must have had the same idea. "We don't know anyone in Keflavíc," she told the man. "Can't we stay here on the boat?"

"Don't be silly!" he said impatiently. "I told you, it's not a safe place for children. Come along, now. Got all your things?"

Before Parsley had time to explain that we hadn't brought any things, I grabbed her hand and said, "There's just my carry-on bag. I'll be right back."

"What carry-on bag?" Parsley asked as I dragged her away.

"Shut up, stupid!" I hissed. "We have to get off this boat and hide somewhere on the island."

At first I thought we'd never get away. The bearded man stood waiting on the pier, smoking a cigarette. The lights were too bright for us to sneak past unobserved. But I guess he got tired of waiting, because he put out his cigarette, swore softly, and climbed back on board to look for us.

"Now's our chance," I whispered.

Slipping through the shadows toward the bow of the boat, we jumped down to the pier and ran.

It was weird, kicking through that volcanic ash. I had imagined it would be light and flaky like the ashes left after a wood fire. Instead, it was granular, like coarse black snow. There were stony lumps in it. Parsley was convinced they were lava bombs, so we each picked one up to keep as a souvenir. They seemed harmless enough on the ground, but when I remembered where they came from, I was filled with dread that one would fall on me.

There were lights in a few of the windows, but mostly the houses loomed up tall and dark on both sides of the street. They kept us from seeing the volcano. We walked in what I thought was the opposite direction and pretty soon came out in the open again, much closer to the volcano than I wanted to be. There were still some houses scattered here and there, but they were abandoned. It grew harder to walk, and the noise became deafening.

"We'd better turn back!" I shouted.

Parsley's eyes were wide open, and her voice trembled. "Owen, look!"

I looked where she was pointing, and jumped back in alarm. The ground just ahead was only a sort of crust, still warm. It was cracked in places, and something orange glowed between the cracks. Not only did it glow, it moved: shifting and seething, like a living thing.

Parsley swirled around in terror and started running back toward the town. I wanted to run too, but my legs and my mind seemed to belong to two different people, and the person with the legs stayed put. That's why I was still there when the Icelandic pony came by. He had a rope dangling around his neck as if he had been tied up but had broken away. And he was galloping wildly toward the volcano.

I remembered the article. Burned and blinded, it

had said. A fireman had taken pity and shot him. Suddenly I knew what it meant. This wasn't just some story in a magazine. This was real. The pony was going to be in terrible pain, and get shot, and die. And scared as I was, I couldn't let it happen.

"Hold it!" I yelled. "Stop!"

I don't know why that worked, but it did. The pony came to a dead halt in front of me and stood panting and sweating, with the glow of the volcano reflected in his frightened eyes. So I reached out and grabbed the rope.

There was a huge explosion. The ground shook, and the air slapped hard against my ears. Rearing up in panic, the pony strained against his rope. I kept hold of the rope with one hand and sheltered my face with the other, thinking for sure we'd both be killed. But everything grew calm again: no glare, no shaking ground, no noise. I was back in the attic room.

And so was the pony.

Parsley was already sitting on the cot. She looked embarrassed. She also looked as if she would rather die than show it.

Pointing her chin defiantly at me she said, "Jeesum, Owen! You're still wearing that man's jacket."

"Want to go back in there and return it?" I asked.

Her pale face turned a little paler, and she shook

her head. "We ought to wash it first," she answered weakly. "It's filthy. Everything you've got on is filthy. You're a mess!"

"Speak for yourself," I said. "You're right, though. We'd better clean up."

Leaving the pony with Flag in the attic, we collected a load of wash and took it downstairs to the machine. I put in the jacket. Parsley added our jeans and the towels we wiped up Flag's messes with. Uncle Jack and Nan-Ellen had spread out the paper on the living-room floor and were looking at the funnies. They didn't notice a thing. Not until the spin cycle, that is.

For me, running the washer is no big deal. I often washed clothes in the basement of our apartment building back in the city. The only time anything went wrong was when I put Canadian quarters in the machine, so I was surprised when the washer started making these deafening thuds, followed by a loud buzzing sound.

Uncle Jack leaped up and came running over. "Load unbalance!" he explained, pushing the button that turns off the machine. "What are you kids up to, anyway?"

Before we had time to answer, he pulled out the jacket and demanded, "Whose is this? Why is it so heavy?"

I tried telling him that the jacket belonged to an

Icelandic fisherman, but he didn't believe me for a minute. Nor was he amused when I said that the large round stone in the pocket was a lava bomb.

Nan-Ellen had gone back to reading the paper, but this made her look up again with sudden interest. "You put a bomb in the washer?"

Uncle Jack's laugh was the annoyed kind, not the kind you laugh when something is funny. He said I hadn't blown up the house yet; I was just practicing.

"This kind of bomb doesn't explode," I explained patiently. "It's a volcanic rock."

Uncle Jack looked at it more closely, and his face lit up. "You know what this really is, Nan-Ellen? I bet this is a geode! If we split it open, there might be amethysts inside."

"It's a lava bomb," I repeated. "Give it back. It's mine."

Uncle Jack handed it over, but not before saying that if there were amethysts inside, he'd sell them to pay for repairing the washer. I could tell he was joking, but Nan-Ellen thought he was dead serious.

"Aren't you being a little unfair?" she asked. "We don't even know if the washer is broken yet. Besides, Owen didn't do it on purpose."

The twinkle faded from Uncle Jack's eyes, and an icy look took its place. He said I had to learn to take the consequences of my actions, whether they were intentional or not. To which my mother replied that learning experience was one thing, and punishment another. Uncle Jack called her overprotective, and another fight began. I tried to change the subject, but I couldn't get a word in edgewise. It was as if I didn't exist and the fight were about something different.

There was nothing wrong with the washer. After we took the rock out, it worked just fine. But when I told Uncle Jack, he wouldn't believe me.

"Oh, yeah? The machine may still be working, but listen to the pipes!"

It's true that the plumbing in that house is noisy. Usually the noise comes from the heater in the basement, though. This time it came from the attic. And there was nothing I could do to keep him from going up to check it out.

Uncle Jack's face was flushed when he got back. "You're not going to believe this," he told Nan-Ellen, "but there's a deer and a horse in our attic."

Parsley corrected him reproachfully. "It's not a horse, Daddy. It's just a pony. Horses have to be fourteen hands or over."

She should have known this wouldn't make things better. In fact, Uncle Jack lost control and began to shout. "I don't care what it is, I want it out of there! Out, do you understand? This is beyond a joke!"

Parsley stuck out her bottom lip.

"How on earth did you get them upstairs?" Nan-Ellen asked. "Where did they come from? How long have they been there, anyway?"

I answered the last question: about half an hour. Which she didn't believe, naturally. How could we have brought Flag and the pony up two flights of stairs without her noticing? So first she lit into me for lying, and next she lit into me for what she called a heartless prank. What's more, she talked as if I had done it to annoy her.

"You ought to know by now how I feel about keeping animals indoors, especially in hot weather!" she said.

It seemed a little unfair for her to put all the blame on me. "What about Parsley's cats? Fourteen of them are still in cages."

"On the sleeping porch," she said. "That's different."

The funny thing is, the more she scolded, the more Uncle Jack looked annoyed. At Nan-Ellen, not at me and Parsley. "When you're raising kids, you've got to be consistent," he lectured. "You make a rule and you carry it through. If you start making exceptions all over the place, you're not doing kids a favor. You're just confusing them."

Nan-Ellen's face turned pink. "What rule? I never made any rules."

"Well, I did," said Uncle Jack. "I said no more

strays, and I meant it. I don't care how late it is; those cats leave the house tonight. And that goes for the horses too."

"They're not horses, Daddy," Parsley repeated patiently. "One's a pony, and one's a deer."

Uncle Jack thought she was being fresh and got really mad. He even grabbed her arm and shook it, which shocked Nan-Ellen. The two of them started yelling at each other, so Parsley and I snuck off for the second time that night.

We were right about horses not liking to go down stairs. We started with the pony and, believe me, it was no easy job. First we tried leading him down. When that didn't work, we tried backing him down. All he did was roll his eyes and kick.

"I know what!" Parsley said, stopping to catch her breath. "Let's blindfold him."

I told her she was nuts. "If he won't move when he can see where he's going, why should he move when he can't?"

"Because what he can't see won't scare him," she reasoned.

At that point, anything was worth a try. I knotted a bandanna over the pony's eyes. He didn't like it, but he let us coax him step-by-step down to the ground floor. After that, Flag was no problem; he followed as if he went down staircases every day of his life. Even so, it was midnight by the time they were settled in the shed. We still had to move the cats.

"I'm glad they're out of the house," I told Parsley as we lugged the last two cages out. "This is only our second day here, and Nan-Ellen is a wreck."

"That was the whole idea, wasn't it?"

"It was a dumb idea," I said. "I never really went along with it."

She shrugged. "The allergy doesn't matter anymore. I bet you guys go home tomorrow."

Tomorrow? I thought about Flag: his trusting eyes, and the warm skin of his neck. I thought about Pip too. "Why tomorrow?"

"They're falling out of love," Parsley whispered gleefully. "Other summers, they never used to fight like this."

"They never used to hug like that either," I said, pointing through the living-room window. "I guess they made up!"

Parsley pulled a long face when she looked in and saw our parents in a clinch. Personally, I felt relieved. Sure, I wanted to move back to Boston. But why the big hurry?

⊱Twelve⊰

I EXPECTED TO SLEEP UNTIL noon the next day. Instead I woke up early with an excited, happy feeling. It took a while before I was awake enough to remember why.

"Flag!" I murmured.

Quickly, I slipped into my jeans and a shirt. Flag would be hungry. I had to find something for him to eat. Corn? We didn't have any, except maybe in the freezer. Cornflakes? Then I laughed at myself. Flag was tame! He would follow me around the way he had followed Jody. I'd take him for a walk out in the field and he could eat grass. We'd go by ourselves, before anyone else woke up.

I was still lacing my sneakers when Nan-Ellen came into my room. "Oh good, you're awake!" she said. "Your uncle wants to talk to you before he leaves for work."

This was a bad sign. I've noticed over the years that when a grown-up wants to talk to me about something good, I don't get summoned. The talk just happens out of the blue. It's only when it's something bad that I'm warned ahead of time.

"What about?" I asked.

"You'll learn soon enough." Suddenly Nan-Ellen noticed Pip. "So you really did have a canary in your room! Why is he in an aquarium? He needs more space."

"Parsley found him. I haven't had time to get him a cage yet."

Nan-Ellen reminded me what Uncle Jack had said about no more strays, but I told her that he meant cats. How could one measly little canary be a problem?

"And Flag—" I stopped. There was no way I could pretend that Flag was little.

She sighed. "It's not just one canary; it's the whole idea of the strays. You'd better hurry on down, because that's what he wants to talk about. Parsley is down there already."

So much for walks in the fields before anyone else was up! I felt kind of foolish.

"He can say what he likes, but I won't give up Flag," I said angrily.

Nan-Ellen didn't answer. She just followed me into the dining room, where Parsley sat, staring sleepy-eyed at a bowl of cereal and milk. Her expression was sulky, so I gathered she had already been talked to.

"I want you to hear this too," Uncle Jack said when I came in. "We're having a wedding tomorrow afternoon, in case you kids have forgotten it. That means guests. Seventeen of them, to be precise. Plus the minister."

"Tomorrow afternoon?" I repeated. I hadn't forgotten, but the reminder gave me quite a jolt. Short of a miracle, I was a Vermonter from now on. Was it too late for a miracle?

"You don't look overjoyed," Uncle Jack told me with a wry smile. "No comment?"

"Does this mean I have to wear a tie?" I asked.

He laughed. "It wouldn't hurt! But that's not the point. The point is, I want those strays out of here before the guests arrive. I don't care how you do it, but I want it done by the time I get back this evening. Otherwise I'll be forced to take drastic measures."

"Like what?" Parsley asked in a frightened whisper.

Uncle Jack twisted his lips nervously before replying, "Like the animal shelter, honey. I'm sorry, but it looks as if this is too much for us to deal with on our own."

Before Parsley had time to protest, Nan-Ellen held up a sheet of paper. "I was afraid it might come to this, so I thought of an alternative. It won't get us results by tomorrow, but if you have it copied at the office, we could post copies around town."

Uncle Jack reached for the flyer and read it aloud:

ATTENTION ANIMAL LOVERS!
Are you lonely? Are you bored?
Have you been secretly longing for
a companion who is loyal, affectionate—
AND WON'T TALK BACK?
FURRY FELINE FRIENDS
Available Now! Free to Good Homes!

At the bottom of the page, Uncle Jack's telephone number was printed vertically fifteen times on little strips that the animal lovers could tear off and take home. It looked very professional. It was also an eye-catcher. If I happened to walk by that notice I'd stop, tear off a strip, and run to the nearest phone.

A wide grin spread across Uncle Jack's face. "The writer's touch!" he said, reaching out to give my mother a hug. "I'm tempted to call our own number and adopt two or three."

It seemed a good moment to appeal to him about

my new pets. "The flyer just says cats. Does that mean I can keep Flag and Pip?"

He shook his head. "Do you realize how much hay we'd need to keep them over the winter? I've solved that problem, though. A fellow from the nature reserve says I can bring him the deer. He'll take the pony too, if no one claims him, but I told him it probably belongs—"

I interrupted him. "Pip is a canary. He eats birdseed, not hay."

Uncle Jack's grin vanished. "You've got until this evening to work out a plan. But it has to be a practical plan or I'm calling the animal shelter first thing in the morning."

No matter how you look at it, this was unfair to me. Granted, I had something to do with bringing Flag and the pony into the house, but not the cats. "What about my book reports?" I argued. "I was hoping you'd drop me off at the library."

This wasn't true, of course. The truth is, I was hoping to spend the day with Flag. But it was as good an excuse as any.

"You don't want to hang out at the library all day," said Uncle Jack. "Just tell me what book you want and I'll pick it up on my way home."

I thought fast. "See if you can find one on volcanos. Something short with big print and a lot of illustrations, okay?"

Nan-Ellen's face lit up at the mention of volcanos. "I know the perfect book! It's called *The Twenty-One Balloons*, and it's one of the best volcano stories ever written. It's about a professor who finds this volcanic island while he's on a balloon trip around the world. Only twenty families live on it. They're all fabulously rich because of the diamond mines, and—"

Parsley's sulky expression turned to one of interest. "Diamonds? Whole mines of them?"

"There are diamonds lying around like cobblestones. The professor stuffs his pockets with some of the smaller ones. He puts them back after a while, though. They make him feel silly."

I've noticed that the more outrageous the story, the more Nan-Ellen's eyes grow big and solemn. They were huge and *very* solemn now, but I could tell that Parsley believed her. "I wouldn't feel silly," she said. "I'd keep them. I want to read that book!"

I knew exactly what she had in mind. "Oh, no you don't! It's for a book report, remember?"

"You can both read it," Nan-Ellen assured us. "I happen to own a copy, so no one has to make a special trip to the library."

Uncle Jack reminded her that the library was across the street from his office. "So I don't mind dropping by if you change your mind. Come to think of it, don't they keep small pets in the children's section? The librarian might take the canary off our hands."

Parsley scowled. "No way! Pip isn't making anybody sneeze. Besides, it would mean I'd have rescued him all for nothing."

"Rescued him from what?" Nan-Ellen asked.

I kicked Parsley under the table, but she answered anyway. "From being starved to death and put in the oven."

The thought of it grossed me out all over again, but Parsley isn't the sensitive type. She just shoved a spoonful of Cheerios into her mouth and chewed.

Uncle Jack gave her a puzzled look. "If you wanted to roast a canary, wouldn't you fatten it up first? Why would someone want to starve it?"

"You don't understand," Parsley mumbled through her Cheerios. "Amy didn't want to eat Pip. It's just she forgot to feed him."

Uncle Jack had been tucking the pad into his briefcase. Now he slammed the case shut as if he were trying to trap the truth in there.

"Finally!" he said. "*Finally* I'm getting the real story. Just who is Amy? Some kid in your school?"

Parsley held the bowl to her mouth and slurped up the last drops of milk. "Amy March, in *Little Women*. She's older than me."

After a moment of stunned silence, Uncle Jack let out a frustrated moan. "See what comes of letting her retreat into books? You deal with her, Nan-Ellen. I've got an early appointment."

If there's one thing that makes Nan-Ellen really mad, it's when people assume that since she works at home, she has an easy schedule. So I wasn't surprised when after finding me *The Twenty-One Balloons*, she disappeared. The only person left to deal with Parsley was me.

"Your father really meant what he said," I told her. "You'd better make your own plan if you want those cats to go to good homes. How about your friends at school?"

Parsley shook her head. "No one would want most of them. The kittens are cute, but the others are too old."

"So take them back where they came from," I said. "I bet their owners miss them like crazy!"

To my surprise, Parsley approved of this solution. In fact, she sat right down to make a list. It seemed like a good time to start my new book, so I retreated to a corner and skimmed through several chapters before she interrupted me.

"I'm stuck," she announced.

"What do you mean? Let's see."

In all that time, this is as far as she'd gotten:

Cat's Name	Cat's Home
Jenny & Pickles	The Fire House

Picky-picky	The Quimbys' house
Garfield	Jon's house
Puss in Boots	Carabas
The Cheshire Cat	Wonderland
Snowball	Stuart Little
Tao	Mr. Longridge

"Forget it," I said. "When your father sees that list, he'll think you've gone crazy. It was bad enough saying you got Pip out of *Little Women*. You want them to take your bookmark away or something?"

Parsley looked blankly at me. "I mean, I don't know about Tao. He nearly drowns in the river. And Snowball wants to kill Stuart Little. Stuart was a mouse, remember?"

I didn't remember because I had never read the book, but I wasn't about to admit it. "If Snowball is a good mouser, why don't we find him a family that has a problem with mice?" I asked.

As soon as the words left my mouth, I realized I had come up with a brilliant idea. The cats didn't all have to go back into the books they came from. Why not switch them around?

"You know who could use a cat?" I continued. "The Ingallses, in *Little House on the Prairie*. I saw that story on TV, and they're nice people. Unless you'd rather take him to those nerds in *Little Women*."

I was just kidding about the March sisters, but Parsley thought I was serious. "You're right! We can do that right now, and bring Pip's cage home while we're at it."

"Hold it!" I said. "If those girls killed their canary, I'd hate to think what they'd do to a cat."

Parsley shook her head impatiently. "They learned a lesson with Pip, right? We can give them Snowball at the end of chapter eleven, where they decide to do chores after all. And you know what? There's a boy named Laurie Laurence who lives next door to the Marches. He's got curly black hair, and big black eyes, and a handsome nose—"

"Yeah? So what?"

"So I bet we could get him to remind them from time to time," Parsley concluded.

Like I said, I'm not much of a reader. But that day, for the first time, I wished I was. There must have been hundreds of better places to take Snowball. Places that I could write about for one of my reports. Because I sure as heck wasn't going to hand in a report about a book called *Little Women*.

"Could we think about this for a while?" I begged. "I don't like the idea of barging into someone's home—especially not an old-fashioned family like that."

Parsley ignored me. "I'll get Snowball and bring him up to my room while you make us some sandwiches. Make a whole bag full, in case they don't feed us there."

I figured she was exaggerating, so I just made two and put them in my pocket. By the time I got back, there was a pile of stuff on Parsley's bed. Looking closely, I saw that it was camping equipment: sleeping bags, a tent, canteens, a flashlight, and even a campstove.

"What's all that for?" I asked suspiciously. "We're not spending the night, are we? Because I'm not going where I haven't been invited."

"Of course not," she said. "I told you; I hate spending the night in other people's houses. That's why we're going to camp out."

"No way!"

Parsley scowled at me. "You want the same thing to happen all over again? We have to make sure they get in the habit of feeding him."

"But you said they'd learned their lesson. And you said Laurie Laurence could remind them to feed Snowball. Right?"

Parsley blushed. "Laurie's my favorite. I like him better than Jo, even. I wouldn't have minded so much if Jo married him, but it's that silly Amy instead. I just don't understand!"

"What does that have to do with how long we stay?" I demanded. "Of all the dumb stories! A boy with a girl's name marries a girl with a boy's name.

So what? I don't see why we have to spend the night."

Parsley turned even pinker. "He marries Amy, not Jo. What I think is, Laurie didn't know many girls. If he got to know a girl like me, it might keep him from making a horrible mistake."

This really cracked me up. "You mean you want him to fall in love with you?"

I guess I shouldn't have laughed. But frankly, the idea of any guy in his right mind falling for my cousin Parsley, age nine, was hilarious. Parsley didn't laugh, though. In fact, she got so close to crying that I asked her to show me the book so I could check it out. I read the whole of chapter 11. Which only convinced me that those March girls were too wimpy to be real, except maybe for Jo.

"What do you see in this stuff?" I asked. "I mean, nothing happens! Jo gets a headache. Amy sits under a bush. All Meg ever does is yawn. And Beth is so blah that I bet her family doesn't notice when she dies. You're not dragging me into a place like that."

Parsley looked teary again. "Please, Owen? This is really important to me. I'll do something for you someday, I promise!"

This gave me an idea. "How about a deal? I'll go with you this time if I get to choose where we go next time. But not overnight, okay? Let's go in on the first morning of their vacation, and then come right back again."

We sat side by side on Parsley's bed. I held Snowball, while she put the bookmark in place. The problem was, Snowball didn't want to be held. Not by me, anyway. He kept yowling and twisting, and I was trying so hard not to get scratched that I didn't look to see the page where Parsley began to read.

"Hurry up, or I'll be permanently scarred," I said. "This guy is a killer!"

Parsley gave me a reproachful look. "Only for mice. I bet he's just too hot here in Vermont."

"That makes two of us," I said. "I hope it's cooler where the March girls live. What time of year do we go in?"

Parsley's face took on a sly expression. "On June first, sometime during the Civil War. Are you ready?"

June first? I had only skimmed chapter 11, but the date rang a bell. "Hey, wait a minute! That's way back at the beginning of the chapter. Doesn't that part happen the night before?"

I made a grab for the book, but it was too late. Opening *Little Women* to the beginning of chapter 11, Parsley read aloud: "*'Three months' vacation — how I shall enjoy it!' exclaimed Meg, coming home one warm day.*"

⇒ *Thirteen* ⇐

IT WAS A *VERY* WARM DAY. Warmer than Vermont in August. I felt the heat even before I felt my bottom hit the floor.

"Jeesum!" said Parsley, whose bottom hit the floor at the same time as mine. "I forgot that the bed would stay in Vermont. What's the matter with Snowball?"

Snowball's hair stood on end. He had dug his claws into my arm, and when I tried to loosen them, he made a sudden wild leap out of my arms to the top of a grandfather clock.

"Don't just sit there!" Parsley snapped at me. "Help me catch him."

I couldn't move. There were three girls in that

parlor. They looked even more prim and proper than in the illustrations, and they were all staring at me. The tall skinny one sat bolt upright on the sofa, her eyes bulging. Her younger sister shrank timidly against her. The oldest of the three, who was kind of overweight, turned pale as if she were about to faint. Not one of them spoke a word.

"That's Jo, and that's Beth, and that's Meg," Parsley said, pointing as she introduced them to me. "Where's Amy?"

Amy was in the doorway, carrying a tray. When I saw her, I was stunned. Why hadn't Parsley mentioned how pretty she was? Like a fairy-tale princess with golden hair, and blue eyes that matched the color of her dress. Plus she had the whitest skin I've ever seen on a girl, even in Boston. Our sudden appearance had made her slosh something onto her dress. She dabbed at the stain with a lacy handkerchief.

"Stop staring, Owen!" Parsley warned me.

I tried to apologize, but I was so embarrassed that all I could do was stutter. Not Parsley, though. You would have thought she was an invited guest, from the way she babbled on.

"We're not burglars," she assured the March sisters. "We're just here on a visit. We came to bring you a cat. You need a cat, don't you?"

Nobody answered, but that didn't bother Parsley.

"I knew you did," she continued confidently. "So I brought you Snowball, and we're only staying long enough to make sure he doesn't starve to death like Pip."

Meg glanced at an empty birdcage by the parlor window, and her face clouded over. "Pip didn't starve. He just disappeared."

"He flew away," Amy added mournfully. "Poor, dear Pip!"

"Flew away?" Parsley looked confused, but only for a moment. "Oh, I get it," she said. "That's what you *guess* happened after I rescued him. For a moment, I mixed up the story with the book."

My warning nudge was a mistake—she thought it meant I didn't understand. "I already told you the difference between a book and a story, Owen. I rescued Pip from the story, remember? But in the book, he still dies."

A tear trickled slowly down Amy's cheek, and she gave a little sob. I was fascinated: Most of the girls I know look awful when they cry. Amy looked prettier.

"There's nothing to cry about now, silly!" Parsley told her scornfully. "Make sure you take good care of Snowball, is all."

How could she be so unfeeling? "Stop it!" I whispered. "Can't you see it's just as bad for them, whether Pip dies or disappears?"

Parsley kept right on talking. "Now that Pip's gone, you don't need the cage anymore. So would it be okay if we took it home with us?"

A chuckle came from a dark corner of the room. I nearly jumped out of my skin. Then I noticed an older woman—probably Mrs. March. I could feel myself blushing.

"I'm sorry," I told her. "Honest! It wasn't my idea. We'll go home right away, I promise."

"Where *is* your home?" asked Mrs. March.

"It's in Vermont," Parsley answered. "Mine is, anyway. Owen may be living there too from now on, but he used to just come for vacations. Real vacations. Not pretend ones like in the book, where you let Pip die."

Mrs. March rose from her chair and started moving toward us.

"Shut up!" I told Parsley. "I'm leaving. You better leave too, before you say something worse."

What I meant was that Pip isn't the only one who dies in the book. Further on, she had told me, Beth dies too. If it made Nan-Ellen cry just reading about it, what would the real thing be like for her family?

Parsley scolded me in a voice that reached across the room. "Don't be such a jerk, Owen! I wouldn't dream of telling them the awful thing that happens to Beth."

A wounded look came into Mrs. March's eyes. I could have killed Parsley! Turning angrily away, I walked out to a dark hallway that was crowded with small tables, mirrors, and an umbrella stand. There I waited, not wanting to lose her in the past. Before long she appeared, glaring defiantly at me and carrying—it took me a moment to identify the bulky thing in the dim light—Pip's cage!

"Are you out of your mind?" I asked. "Put that back where you got it."

"We need it more than they do."

I tried to grab it away from her, but Parsley is quick. She slipped past me and was halfway to the front door before I knew what had happened.

"It's stealing!" I called after her. "If you don't leave that here, I'll tell your father!"

I still think we might have gotten away with our visit if we had just left quietly. But suddenly the sisters came to life. Amy fluttered into the hallway shrieking, "Stop, thief!" Jo followed, snatching up the nearest weapon, which happened to be a silver-handled cane. I didn't wait to see what she meant to do with it.

"Run, Parsley!" I yelled.

Parsley ran. She didn't get far, though: The front door was a heavy, old-fashioned one, and she didn't manage to yank it open until Meg had grabbed her by the seat of her jeans. She broke free, but it was

143

too late. Coming up the walk was a teenaged boy with curly black hair, big black eyes, and a handsome nose. He held a bunch of flowers in one hand. At the sight of Parsley, he flung the flowers aside and tried to block her way. Which was no problem, since Parsley stood still and beamed at him.

What about me? I slipped away easily, in all that commotion. I know it wasn't very loyal of me to desert Parsley, but loyal happened to be the exact opposite of how I felt. She had agreed not to barge into the Marches' home, and not to spend the night. Then she went and broke her word on both points! She was the most self-centered kid I had ever known, and I didn't want her as my sister. She could be Laurie Laurence's sister instead, for all I cared, and spend her life in *Little Women*. I wished I could bring Amy home with me instead.

When I say I slipped away, I mean only as far as a hedge that separated the Marches' house from the house next door. At first it had seemed impenetrable, but inside, it was hollow like a cave. I decided to hide there for a while. Maybe even until the bookmark took me home. At least I had the sandwiches! While I ate one, I indulged in a private fantasy where Laurie Laurence locked Parsley up in a closet full of spiders. It would serve her right for tricking me.

For ages, nothing happened. I strained my ears, but I couldn't hear a sound from the Marches' house. I got so bored that I ate the other sandwich. At last the front door opened again, and Laurie came out. He was smiling to himself as he strolled down the narrow flagstone walk, stopping from time to time to admire the flowers that bordered it. I had had plenty of time to look at those flowers myself. They were pretty: mostly shades of pink, and swarming with bees. Which sister took care of the garden, I wondered? Maybe Amy!

Laurie stooped to pick a flower. He twiddled the stem between his fingers and brushed it against his nose. Still smiling, he murmured, "Parsley!"

Could he have fallen for her after all? With Amy in the house? I put him down as crazy until I heard him add, "What a silly little goose!"

I laughed in spite of myself, but froze again when Laurie dropped the flower and moved in my direction. He must have heard me. He was walking faster now, with a purposeful look on his face. And I could have sworn he was staring straight at me.

"This is where they break for the commercial," I told myself, sweating with panic. "One minute you're thinking murder, the next you're thinking Diet Pepsi. *Where's the commercial?*"

I got into a crouching position, ready to spring through the hedge and run for it. "Not yet," I told myself. "Not while he's got his eye on you. Wait until he looks away! Wait—wait—"

He didn't look away, not even for a second. But just as I was set to break shelter, he disappeared. Where to? The only place he could have gone was into the hedge like me, but I heard no rustling leaves or snapping twigs. Only footsteps, and they were growing fainter now. Twisting around, I peered through the far side of the hedge. What I saw was Laurie's back. When he reached the house next door, he went inside.

"That's where he lives," I thought. "There must be an opening in the hedge. Way to go, Owen: Give yourself a heart attack for nothing!"

It was growing dark. One by one, windows lit up in the Marches' house. The light came from oil lamps, I guessed; during the Civil War, people had no electricity. The March girls couldn't watch TV. They probably read a lot instead, like Parsley. Maybe one of them was reading aloud right now, by the light of an oil lamp. The other three would be listening. With their mother, of course. And Parsley. All of a sudden, I felt sorry for myself. *I* hadn't done anything wrong. Why should I wait in the hedge while the March family entertained Parsley? I could no longer kid myself about spiders and closets. More likely, she was having the time of her life.

146

There had been a breeze when I first came outside, but now the air was muggy and still. The
mosquitos were awful. I yawned, and scratched,
and yawned some more. Hours went by. I fell
asleep once, but not for long. What finally decided
me to move was Snowball. He must have smelled
me or something, because he leaped through the
branches, landing on my lap.

"Ready to go back to Vermont?" I whispered.
"Me too, but you're staying right here. It'll be hard
enough finding homes for all the rest."

Holding him tight in my arms, I tiptoed toward
the house. The windows had been left open, and it
wouldn't hurt to look inside. If everyone had gone
to bed, maybe I could doze on a sofa for a while. If
not, I could always go back to the hedge. But all
was silent, except for the ticking of the grandfather
clock. I was on the point of climbing in when
someone else climbed out.

"Where have you been all night?" asked Parsley.

You'd think I would have had the sense not to
make a scene right by the window, but I couldn't
help myself. I told Parsley how awful it was inside
the hedge, and how it was her fault. Then I said
what I thought of kids who promise one thing and
do another. I ended up by mentioning how rude
she had been in the Marches' parlor.

"Couldn't you tell how peaceful they were before

we came?" I asked. "And suddenly there we are with Snowball making all that noise. And we worry Mrs. March, and make Amy cry—"

Parsley interrupted me. "Amy deserves to cry! She's a nitwit, and I consider her personally responsible for killing Pip."

I started to protest, but Parsley drowned me out with this really fake-sounding giggle. "Owen's in love with Amy!" she chanted. "Owen's in love with a girl in a book!"

"Oh, yeah? Look who's talking! How did you get along with Laurie Laurence, since we're on the subject? Has he proposed to you yet? I don't see any engagement ring."

My aim was to make Parsley good and mad. Instead, she burst into tears. I can't say it gave me much satisfaction.

"Hey, wait a minute!" I said. "What's the problem? It can't have been that bad."

Between sobs, Parsley told me the whole story. No one had locked her into a closet. No one had even been angry. Instead they had questioned her gently, which she claimed was worse.

"What do you mean, worse?" I asked. "It sounds nice enough to me."

"They laughed at me! Laurie thought I was *funny*. And he wouldn't believe me when I said I was a girl. He said that girls wear dresses."

"This is over a century ago," I reminded her. "Back in Laurie's time, even boys didn't wear jeans and T-shirts. I bet they didn't exist."

Parsley's voice rose hysterically. "I told him that! I told him I was from the future, but he said I was a little goose."

I refrained from mentioning that Laurie had said it again, out on the garden walk. She was upset enough as it was. "Calm down!" I begged her.

I watched this talk show once on TV about how when quiet people lose their cool, they have a lot more trouble than people who lose it all the time. Parsley proved this to be true. Instead of calming down, she began to scream.

"Laurie Laurence is a scumball! Laurie Laurence is a jerk!"

A window rattled open over our heads, and Mrs. March peered down, wearing a frilly nightcap. A moment later, all four of her daughters appeared at her side. Before they could do more than stare, a door slammed on the far side of the hedge. Laurie Laurence came racing toward us in silky white pajamas that flapped under the hem of a silky dressing gown. His hair was still tousled from sleep, and his cheeks were flushed. I would have laughed if it weren't for the look in his eyes—it was ferocious.

"You nasty little vagabonds!" he said. "Just wait till I get hold of you!"

149

"Run, Parsley!" I yelled for the second time that day.

This time, Parsley didn't run. Why not? Because she had just noticed Amy, whose hair was tied up in a million strips of rag. I have to admit that she looked bizarre—as if a cloud of limp butterflies had landed on her head. After one startled glance, Parsley quit screaming and let out a whoop of laughter.

"Run!" I repeated, tugging at her arm. "We've got to hide! The bookmark won't take us home until tomorrow morning."

Still laughing, Parsley pointed over my shoulder. "But Owen, look at the sun—it *is* tomorrow morning!"

In the last moment before Laurie tackled me, I glanced back and saw a square of light above the trees.

"The sun isn't square, you idiot!" I said as I toppled over on the lawn.

Only it was Parsley's bed, not the lawn. And the square of light was Parsley's window.

⇢⇢*Fourteen*⇠⇠

"OF ALL THE SNEAKY, SELFISH, snot-nosed little creeps, you take the cake!"

Parsley's mouth dropped open. "Me?"

"Yes, you! All you ever think of is yourself. It's Parsley, Parsley, Parsley, all the time. You were horrible to those people!"

"They weren't real," she said. "You know that."

"Well, that doesn't mean they don't have feelings, does it?"

She giggled, and I couldn't blame her. It sounded pretty silly. But I was right, just the same. Laurie, Mrs. March, and the four sisters all had feelings, and Parsley had no business treating them the way she did.

"If you think they don't have feelings, how come you're so crazy about the book?" I asked.

"I've changed my mind about the book," Parsley admitted. "I didn't know how silly they were."

"Including Laurie?"

"Laurie was silly too. I'm glad he marries Amy in the end! When two people are as silly as that, they deserve each other."

I could see I wasn't getting anywhere with *Little Women*, so I changed my angle of attack. "You're horrible to real people too."

"Like who?"

"Like me, for instance. And my mother. You don't care one bit about all those cats you brought home. You didn't even remember to feed them yesterday. You know who fed them? My mother, that's who, and she's allergic."

A sulky expression clouded Parsley's face. "That's the whole point."

"Well, it's a really dumb point," I said, forgetting that the day before, I had approved of it. "It's not going to work. I don't even want it to work. If Nan-Ellen is happy here, she should get to stay."

Parsley had the nerve to look me straight in the eyes and say, "Daddy doesn't love her!"

Something boiled up inside me. I'd been trying to keep a handle on my temper, but this time she went too far. "Are you kidding? He's crazy about her!" My voice came out in an embarrassingly high warble, I was so angry. "She's pretty, and she's famous, and she's nice to people. You're afraid he doesn't love *you*, is what you mean!"

I'll never forget the look that came into Parsley's eyes. I may never forgive myself for it, either. You don't yell at kids for hurting people's feelings one minute, and the next minute turn around and hurt theirs.

"Oh, relax!" I said, beginning to wish I'd kept my mouth shut. "I didn't mean it. You know your father loves you, no matter how awful you are."

This didn't help. Parsley flung herself face downward on her bed, right on top of those camping supplies that never made it into *Little Women*. Even muffled, the sounds that came out of her were impressive.

"You're not all that bad, actually," I said reluctantly. "I mean, you're smart, and you can be good company. Sometimes. I'm not surprised Nan-Ellen wants to write about you."

Parsley rolled over and squinted at me. Her eyes were red and puffy. "How come she never writes about *you*?"

One of my shoelaces was undone. It seemed like a good time to tie it again.

"Because you're not smart, and you're not good company?"

If Parsley had said that in her usual smart-alecky way, I would have socked her one. But there was a note of sympathy in her voice that saved her. I still didn't answer.

"You know your mom loves you, no matter how awful you are," she mimicked.

Looking up from my sneaker, I saw a wide grin on her face.

"You asked for it!" I said, and I heaved a pillow at her.

Parsley heaved one back. It wasn't until little bits of foam rubber started flying around the room that we stopped the fight. By that time, we were both laughing.

"We'd better pick this stuff up," said Parsley. "Look at the rug!"

I looked, which is how I noticed the books that were lying there.

"*The Fledgling*," I said, reading off the titles. "*The Wonderful Adventures of Nils*. Are you reading both of these at once?"

"Not really. I'm choosing where to go, is all."

Reaching for one of them, I flipped quickly through the pages. "Is this any good?"

"They're both good. I want to go into *The Twenty-One Balloons* first, though, and bring home a diamond for my collection."

"That would be stealing," I reminded her. But I

was trying to make peace, not start another quarrel, so I changed the subject. "Speaking of *The Twenty-One Balloons*, I'd better finish reading it if I want to do my report on it."

"Why bother?" Parsley asked temptingly. "Why don't we just go there?"

I told her that the first volcano was scary enough. I wanted to find out just how bad this one was before we paid it a visit. "I'll be in my room if you need me," I concluded.

"Why would I need you? While you're doing that, I'm going to ride a goose."

I was halfway out the door, but I came back fast. "You're going to what?"

"I'm going to fly on a goose. Won't that be exciting, Owen? I can't wait!"

"Hold it!" I said. "You mean really fly, up in the air?"

Parsley wiped her nose on her pillow case. "The problem is, I can't decide which goose: the one Nils rode, or the one in *The Fledgling*. Which would you choose?"

"Neither," I said. "Listen, Parsley, flying isn't safe. You're too heavy to ride on birds. I saw the movie about Nils on TV, and he shrinks a lot first."

"Georgie doesn't shrink, in *The Fledgling*. You can come too, if you like."

She handed me a book with a girl and a Canada

goose both flying on the cover. I opened it and read a page. Then I got interested and skimmed through the first three chapters.

"It says Georgie is small for her age," I argued. "She wears red overalls, for Pete's sake! She's just a little kid."

"So am I."

Was Parsley really dumb enough to try a stunt like that? "You're out of your mind," I said. "You'd fall off and kill yourself."

She shook her head stubbornly. "No, I wouldn't."

"If you start doing crazy things like that, I'll tell your father."

Parsley shrugged. "Tell him what? That we have a magic bookmark? He wouldn't believe you."

"I'd make him believe me. I'd prove it."

"And then what?" she demanded. "He'd call the police, or something. Is that what you want?"

A horrible thought came into my head. What if it got around that two kids had found a way to go into books, just like something out of a sci-fi movie? News would spread. Some grown-up would confiscate our bookmark, and the next thing you knew, Parsley and I would be on some nationwide talk show. Back in Boston, I might have liked the idea. Not anymore. I'd had enough of prying into other people's lives, and I wanted no one prying into mine.

"No," I admitted. "That's not what I want."

Taking *The Fledgling* away from me, Parsley reached for her bookmark. "It's September in this chapter," she informed me. "Georgie rides on the Goose Prince just before dawn. That's before he teaches her to fly alone. It says in the book how she reaches back inside the window for Eddy's jacket, so it must be cold. I'm bringing a sweater. You better bring one too."

"No way!" I said. "I haven't recovered from *Little Women* yet."

But it was too late. *"His gentle hooting woke her before dawn,"* Parsley read hastily. In an instant we were there, and she was right; it was cold in Georgie's bedroom. Icy cold.

"Damn it!" I gasped. "Couldn't you have asked me first?"

Parsley laid a warning hand on my shoulder. "Shhh! She'll hear you."

A child stood at the window, staring lovingly at a dark silhouette outside. She was barefoot and, like Laurie Laurence, wearing pajamas. She would already have heard me if it weren't for the tapping on the windowpane. Shoving the window up, she whispered, "Oh, hello there!" She was talking to the Goose Prince, not to us.

I shivered and hugged my arms around me while I watched. Why wasn't Georgie cold? She seemed so frail. Much frailer than it said in the book. But the yearning inside her was strong; I was sure of that. She cared about the Goose Prince as much as Jody cared about Flag.

"This is wrong," I whispered. "We shouldn't have come here."

Parsley ignored me. "Now!" she said, springing to her feet as Georgie climbed out on the roof.

I grabbed her arm. "Are you crazy? Leave her alone!"

Parsley is a wiry little kid. I knew I couldn't hold her back for long. She struggled and kicked, and even tried to bite me. But I managed not to let go until I saw Georgie straddle the goose and settle herself with her arms around his neck.

There was a rattling sound as the goose tried to gain his balance on the shingles. Just when I was sure he would fall to the ground, he sprang forward from the roof's edge. The heaving of his wings seemed too slow to lift the two of them, but miraculously he rose. Over the bushes, over the rooftop and the trees. I held my breath until he was far away, heading toward the narrow crescent moon in the predawn sky.

"Georgie is crazy too," I said. "Totally bonkers. But you've got to agree she's brave!"

Parsley didn't answer. With an angry cry, she tore away from my grasp. Before I could stop her, she had scrambled through the window and was on the roof, screaming, "Wait! Wait for me!"

I moved as fast as I could, but it wasn't fast enough. There was another rattling sound, much louder than the one the Goose Prince had made. Parsley whimpered and then screamed again, this time with terror. After, there was only silence.

Was she dead? How far was it to the ground? Hurrying back toward the bedroom door, I nearly ran into a woman in a nightgown. She looked terrified.

"Who are you?" she demanded breathlessly. Before I could answer, she added, "Did Georgie fall off that bird?"

I tried to explain that it was Parsley who had fallen. Off the roof, not off the Goose Prince. But my voice kept squeaking instead of making words.

The woman grabbed my hand. "Come with me. Hurry!"

I followed her down a hallway, then down a flight of stairs. She led me to a door, which she flung open. Together, we ran out on the lawn. The grass was wet with dew and strewn with dark patches of fallen leaves.

"Parsley will be lying in the grass," I thought. "Parsley will be dead."

"Thank God!" the woman said suddenly as we rounded the corner of the house. "We left a big leaf pile under that window."

If I hadn't been so scared, I would have laughed. Parsley was half buried. There were leaves in her hair, up her sleeves, everywhere. She wasn't badly hurt, just scratched up. But she had been as scared as I was, there was no doubt about that. With her pale face and big, frightened eyes, she looked as frail as Georgie.

"You could have killed yourself," I said, feeling slightly sick.

Parsley's bottom lip quivered. The woman looked as if she wanted to hug her, but was holding back out of—I don't know, some mixture of understanding and respect. "You'd better both come inside and warm up," she said quietly. "I'm Georgie's mother."

She had a stern type of face, but when she smiled, it made me feel warm all over. I liked her a lot. I had this weird feeling that whatever I said to her, she wouldn't be surprised or shocked. So when she asked who we were and where we came from, I told the truth.

"You came here through a book," she murmured thoughtfully. "Why not? Houses aren't the only things with windows. Time and space may well have them too."

She had made us each a cup of hot chocolate, which we drank sitting at the kitchen table. If that table hadn't been between us, I think I would have thrown my arms around her. "Georgie is lucky!" I said.

A doubtful look shadowed her face. "Is she? I wonder. She wants to fly. I didn't stop her, but perhaps I should. Did your mother try to stop you?"

"My mother doesn't know where we are," I said.

"And my mom is dead," Parsley added flatly.

I expected the woman to console Parsley, but I guess that wasn't her style. Instead, she gazed into her eyes and took a sip of hot chocolate. Neither of them spoke, but it was a comfortable silence. Then Parsley walked slowly around the table and climbed onto the woman's lap, where she began to cry—quiet tears that kept on coming, as if she had been saving them up since my aunt Lyle died. I could understand why she did it. I just wished she had more time before Georgie's mother and her kitchen disappeared, and we were back home again.

"Are you okay?" I asked, feeling shy.

Parsley was still holding her cup. She carried it carefully to the shelf where she kept her souvenirs. Then she turned and scowled at me. "Of course I'm not okay! You spoiled it. I didn't get to fly after all, and it's your fault."

That was too much! "You're the one who put the bookmark in," I pointed out. "I didn't even know we were going. You didn't warn me."

161

"Well, I'm warning you now. I'm going back, and this time I'm going to have *fun*."

"Fun!" I repeated indignantly. "You're supposed to be finding homes for the cats, not having fun."

Parsley brightened up. "I'll give the three little kittens to Georgie's mother. I could give her *all* the cats. I bet she'd take really good care of them."

"You just want to sit on her lap again," I teased.

She glared at me. Then her shoulders slumped and her bottom lip began to quiver all over again. It had been a tearful day for Parsley.

"Don't!" I said. "Don't cry. I know how you feel."

"How can you? *Your* mom is still alive."

"You can share her," I said, although I knew it wouldn't be the same.

Parsley knew it too. "She's not the lap-sitting type."

"She's okay," I said. "Not very lap-sitting, but okay. If you go downstairs, she'll help you put something on those scratches."

Parsley walked over to the mirror and studied her reflection lengthily. I didn't think nine-year-olds cared much about appearance, but she proved me wrong. Turning this way and that, she made little whimpering noises, as if she were scarred for life. At first it was funny, but it went on for a long time. So long that I stopped watching and began looking around the room instead. That's when I saw the bookmark. It had fallen out of *The Fledgling* and was lying by the door.

Could she see me in the mirror? I reached for the bookmark, ready to draw my hand back if she turned around.

"Jeesum!" said Parsley. "Do I ever look terrible! What's Daddy going to say?"

"Maybe he won't notice," I suggested, slipping the bookmark into my pocket. "You'd be surprised at how many things people don't notice."

"Not me," said Parsley. "I notice everything."

But as far as I knew, she didn't notice when I left the room.

⇶Fifteen⇷

BACK IN MY OWN ROOM, I felt totally wiped out. I didn't want to travel anywhere for a long time. Except maybe down to the brook for a quick dunk, all on my own. In Boston, I was on my own most of the time. That is, there were millions of people around, but they didn't bother me. Here in Vermont where I couldn't even see another house from my window, I never had a moment to myself.

It's funny how powerful I felt with the bookmark in my pocket. It was a new feeling, and one that I enjoyed. "Why not stay all day at the brook?" I asked myself. "Those cats are Parsley's problem, not mine. I have work to do."

I reached for *The Twenty-One Balloons*. But

where was my bathing suit? I looked around the room for it and finally found it under my bed. *The Yearling* was there too. It must have lain there since I cried over the chapter where Jody shoots Flag. I picked it up, telling myself that I'd have plenty of time to read for both reports, down at the brook.

The thought of Flag troubled me, though. Was Uncle Jack serious about the nature reserve? Wouldn't Flag be lonely there? I stopped at the shed to check on him and found Nan-Ellen. In one hand she was holding a basket full of dark green leaves. With the other, she was stroking the Icelandic pony.

"What are you trying to do—work up an asthma attack?" I asked. "I thought the whole point of moving the cats out here was so you'd be away from them!"

She smiled. "I just dropped in to say 'hi' to this little fellow. I was gathering comfrey."

"What the heck is comfrey?"

"It's kind of like spinach," she explained. "It's used a lot for folk medicine, but I've heard it's good to eat, too. There's tons of it, all around this shed. Want to help me pick it?"

"I have to work on my reports," I said, hiding my bathing suit behind my back.

Nan-Ellen nodded approvingly and asked how I liked *The Twenty-One Balloons*. When I said I liked it fine, she began telling me all over again what a great book it was.

I interrupted her. "Talking of books, have you ever read *The Fledgling?*"

She wrinkled her brow. "I don't think so. What's it about?"

"It's about this kid who flies on a goose. Have you read *The Wonderful Adventures of Nils?*"

"Of course. Why, Owen?"

I decided to level with her, up to a point. "Nils flies on a goose too. Parsley is reading both of them. What do you think would happen to Parsley if she tried to fly? Wouldn't she get hurt?"

Nan-Ellen shrugged. "I suppose so. That's the magic of fiction, isn't it? The reader can take risks that in real life—"

She rambled on for a while, and I listened politely. I mean, she's a famous writer, and this was hardly the time to discourage her. But after a few minutes she stopped and said, "Just what is it that's worrying you?"

So I leveled with her a little bit more, to see how she would take it. "Parsley really believes she can fly. She's got this bookmark that says a story can take you anywhere for free, and she really thinks it can happen."

Nan-Ellen smiled. "That's sweet."

"It's not sweet, it's dangerous! Someone should take those books away from her. I've already taken the bookmark away. But watch me get in trouble for it later."

The trouble came right then and there. Nan-Ellen told me I was too free with advice for other people's lives. "Besides," she added, "think of the millions of children all over the United States who are glued to a TV set right this very moment! Let Parsley play her book games, and stop trying to organize the child."

Organize? How unfair could you get? I changed the subject. "You're not serving comfrey at the reception tomorrow, are you? I thought you were going to have it catered."

Nan-Ellen shook her head. "There are no caterers around here, so it's potluck. We asked the guests to bring stuff."

"That sounds like a good idea," I said. "You're probably too busy with number thirty-one to cook anyway. What chapter are you on?"

Instead of answering, Nan-Ellen offered a leaf of comfrey to the pony. This worried me. Would she become so obsessed with country life that she stopped writing altogether? That would be a terrible mistake, and I could see it was my job to point it out to her. I started by saying how it was nice being close to nature and all, but summer was almost over.

"So?" she asked.

I took a deep breath. "So maybe it's time to sit down and start that new book instead of wasting your energy on weird vegetables that not one single person besides you in this family can even look at without puking."

Nan-Ellen gave me an outraged look. "For your information, I've written thirty pages."

"About Parsley?" I asked.

Nan-Ellen shook her head. "About Owen."

"Me?"

"Know any other Owens? You don't mind, do you? I'll call you something else, naturally. And is it all right if I make you a little younger? Seventh grade is too grown up for what I have in mind."

When I asked what she had in mind, she began to pace the shed with the familiar dreamy look on her face, just like the night she told me about getting remarried and moving to Vermont. Except this time, the dreamy look was for me.

"I have in mind this kid who has to make a big adjustment. Like us: divorce in one family, death in the other, and then a marriage between the two."

"What happened to funny?" I asked.

"Forget funny. This book is going to be serious. The whole scene is tough on the kid, naturally, and he thinks he can't deal with it. But he's stronger than he thinks. He's kind of the caretaker of the family, see?"

"Just so long as you don't mean baby-sitter," I said. "Because I've been meaning to tell you: I'm through with baby-sitting. Finished. Parsley can break her neck if she likes, but I refuse to be responsible."

She couldn't have heard me. At least, she didn't react. Instead she started talking about how I was the responsible type, which was news to me. She reminded me how I looked after her before Uncle Jack took over the job, and how upset I was to think she didn't need me anymore, so I transferred my caretaking energy to this pet deer, and was going to keep it through the winter in a tumbledown shed.

"Except I think we should fix up the shed," she said. "It doesn't look as if it will make it through another Vermont winter."

I was on the point of objecting to her description of me, but these last words caught my attention. "Through the winter?" I repeated. "You mean I get to keep Flag?"

Her eyes sparkled with excitement. "Won't it make a wonderful story? I'll have to call him something else, of course. That name's been used in a book already. A really good book—you should read it someday."

When I told her I had already read parts of *The Yearling*, she was so surprised that it was insulting.

But I have to hand it to her, she pulled herself together fast and asked what I thought of the book.

"I like it," I admitted. "I'm thinking of using it for one of my reports. Only it's sad! I hate Ma Baxter. How could she shoot Flag? You'd never do a thing like that, would you?"

Nan-Ellen gave my question her full attention. She explained how I should try to see it from a farmer's point of view. The Baxters were poor. Each time Flag got into their crops, it meant winter days when they'd go hungry. They couldn't afford to feed an animal that wasn't earning its keep.

She was right. Parsley had told me how all the corn went to their cow or to old Caesar, their horse. "I suppose if Jody had taught Flag to pull a plow, his parents wouldn't have complained about him," I said bitterly.

"Not as much, anyway," Nan-Ellen agreed. "It's a pity that Jody couldn't keep him as a pet, but pets are a luxury."

I told her it was a pity Flag wasn't a horse, because then he could be a pet *and* useful. "I bet this pony could pull a plow," I said. "Jody could ride him to town, too."

I meant it as sort of a joke, but it put an idea into my head. A really weird idea. I wasn't sure it would work, but what did I have to lose?

⇥Sixteen⇤

MY IDEA CONCERNED FLAG. Not the Flag who was safe in Vermont, but the one in the story who gets killed at the end. If I went back, would he be there or not?

According to Parsley's theory, he wouldn't. We couldn't change a book, she had said, but we could change a story, because stories are alive. It looked as if she was right in the case of *Little Women*, because when she visited the March family for the second time, Pip was gone. Did that mean we had changed the story of *The Yearling* too? I intended to find out.

In chapter 32, after the part in the clearing where we went in, Jody wanders off with Flag and doesn't get home until after dark. This time I'd go in a little later, straight to Jody's home. If the story hadn't changed, I'd see Flag galloping across the yard, which would mean that the next day, he would still get shot. If we *had* rescued Flag, Jody would come home alone. He'd feel sad, of course, but not for long. Because I was bringing him the pony.

I was dazzled by the brilliance of my plan. It worked out well for everyone! By a stroke of luck, I even had the book and bookmark with me. There was only one question: Would the pony cooperate? As soon as my mother left the shed, I tried to explain things to him. I thought this would reassure him, even if he couldn't understand. Unfortunately, it had the opposite effect. Maybe he sensed that I was nervous. In any case, he started making this wheezy noise, and did a kind of tap dance to get away from me.

"Quiet, boy!" I crooned. "Whoa, boy!"

It was no easy job getting a grip on his halter. I began to panic: What if Parsley found me in the shed? Would she want to come along? Luckily, the pony calmed down enough for me to to slip a rope through a ring on his halter. Holding tight to the end of this rope, I opened *The Yearling* and placed the bookmark next to page 408. Then I flipped back a few pages, propped the open book against a pile of flower pots, and began to read:

He reached Baxter's Island after dark—

This time, the change was so rapid that I felt stunned. Rays of sunlight had filtered through the boards of the old shed, back in Vermont. Here in the Baxters' yard it was nighttime, with no moon at all. The air was humid and warm, as if it had just rained or was about to rain. There was no sign of Jody. Was that good or bad? I crept close to a window and looked in. There was Ma Baxter, sewing her patchwork pieces by candlelight just like the book said. And there beside her, looking numb and pale, was Jody.

I've seen movies that had me close to tears, but even the saddest of them was nothing compared to this. Jody was hurting. I could tell! And I hurt with him: a tight, heavy kind of hurt that swelled inside my chest and behind my jaw. What did it mean? Was it because Flag was still there and condemned to die? Should I knock on the door and ask? Before I could decide, the dogs began to bark. A voice shouted at Jody to see what they had scented. What they had scented was me and the Icelandic pony.

I had been sure that when we arrived in Florida, the pony would get scared and bolt. To my surprise, he remained calm. He didn't whinny, or stamp his hoofs, or do anything that would bring Jody's parents to the door. Jody himself was the only one to step out into the night. When he recognized me, he shut the door behind him.

"Where's Flag?" he demanded.

I nearly fainted with relief. So we *had* changed the story! Jody's grief was due to missing the yearling, and I had a cure for that. Or did I? "He's safe," I said. "I promised, remember?"

Jody nodded. He looked gloomy and resigned. This was the moment to hand over the pony, but for some reason I hesitated. Back in Vermont, I had thought it would be easy. Easy and fun! Now I wasn't sure. Could Jody really stop loving one pet and start right in loving another?

"See this pony?" I began.

That was dumb. Of course Jody saw the pony. He seemed uninterested, though. What if he didn't want him? Maybe he didn't want a pet at all, if he couldn't have Flag.

"He's for you," I said, forcing myself to pursue my plan. "I knew you'd miss Flag, so I brought him. Here, take him!"

Jody stepped backward and shook his head.

"Please! I know he won't be the same as Flag, but he's better than no pet at all, and he can work for you."

"Jody!" a voice called from inside. "Is someone out there, boy?"

"That's Ma!" Jody told me, and he called back to say nothing was out there, nothing at all.

At least he wasn't bringing his parents into this. I considered it a good sign.

"Caesar is getting pretty old, isn't he?" I asked. "What will you and your father do for a horse when he dies? This pony can pull a plow. He's strong."

Again, he shook his head.

Why couldn't Jody see things my way? I began to feel desperate. For the first time in my life, I realized how frustrating it can be when you think you're doing someone a favor and they don't agree.

Then I had an idea. "I'm in trouble, see. With my uncle. He says we can't keep the pony, but I thought he'd be safe with you. And listen, I can help with his feed if things get rough."

This hadn't occurred to me before, but it was my day for good ideas. If I had brought the pony in, I could bring other things in too. Oats, for instance, or whatever ponies eat. It would be a drain on my allowance, but Florida winters don't last long. I figured he could mostly go out and eat grass.

It was too dark to see Jody's expression, but I sensed that we had come to some sort of understanding. So I waited. Waited quietly, not trying to pressure him while he made up his mind. But my heart beat fast with uncertainty until he reached out and took the rope.

"Jody!" the voice called again. "What are you doing out there, boy?"

This time, he didn't answer. Not his mother, I mean. He answered me instead. "I'll do it," he said. "As a favor to you, I'll do it."

As a favor? I had expected him to be grateful! A resentful feeling rose up in me, but it vanished a moment later. Candlelight shone on Jody's face as he led the pony past a window. His face was happy. His voice was happy too when he turned and whispered, "Thanks!"

Then it all disappeared: the candlelight, the house, the pony, the boy. Even the heavy, hurt feeling was gone. I was back home again, and I felt wonderful. After all, how often do you get to change someone's life for the better? Nan-Ellen was right when she said I was a caretaker. I had taken care of Jody, and we were both happier. Jody's happiness wasn't written in the book, but I knew about it. Me and nobody else in the entire world, as long as I kept my secret.

Unfortunately, I didn't keep it long. I let it out that evening, in the middle of a four-way family fight. It was a pointless fight: the kind that switches from one thing to another without ever touching the important issue. But by the time it's over, everyone is a wreck. It started when Uncle Jack came home from work and stumbled over Garfield. I don't know how he got out. Parsley said it was because I left the shed door open, but he had been in a cage. Who had opened the cage? I suspected Parsley.

"That cage was shut when I was in the shed," I told her.

"Why were you in the shed?"

I reminded her that this was my place too, since our parents were getting married. I could go wherever I liked. We bickered for a few minutes, which gave Uncle Jack time to put down his briefcase and pick up a sheet of paper that lay on the floor. After he read it, he was silent for a while. So silent that Parsley and I quit bickering and started to wonder what was going on. That's when Nan-Ellen walked in and joined the fun.

"Welcome home, honey!" she said, giving Uncle Jack a big, juicy smack on the cheek. "Have I ever got a surprise for you!"

Uncle Jack didn't ask her what it was. Instead, he looked up from the piece of paper and stared coldly at me and Parsley. "Is this a joke?"

We didn't know what he meant until he read aloud: "'Puss in Boots, Carabas. The Cheshire Cat, Wonderland. Snowball, Stuart Little. Tao, Mr. Longridge'—what kind of nonsense is this?"

In the excitement of taking the pony into *The Yearling*, I had totally forgotten Parsley's plan. No wonder he was angry; he thought we were playing games!

"I can explain," I said, which was nonsense too.

Uncle Jack said he wanted results, not explanations. He said we'd had plenty of time to find homes for the strays. He told us he was a patient man, but we had pushed him to his absolute limit. When he stopped to catch his breath, Nan-Ellen announced that I was keeping Flag so she could write a book about a boy with a pet deer. I didn't think it was a good time to bring the subject up. I still don't.

Uncle Jack crumpled Parsley's plan into a ball and tossed in into the fireplace. "Damn it! Why can't you consult me before you make these crazy decisions?"

"I am consulting you," Nan-Ellen said.

"You're informing me. Apparently you informed Owen first. Where do I come into the so-called consultation? Can you tell me that?"

All Nan-Ellen told him was "Please don't shout."

He hadn't actually been shouting yet. But after she said it, he began shouting at her. I don't remember what he was accusing her of. All I remember is that she got bright red.

"You're nothing but a bully!" she said, her voice trembling. "The children have found a home for one of the cats already. Why can't you congratulate them, instead of making all this commotion?"

"I found a home for the pony too," I added before remembering that I'd meant to keep it secret.

Both parents were impressed. They wanted to know about the home, naturally, so I said it was with its rightful owner. This was only a partial lie. I mean, who else but Jody did the pony belong to? The problem was that Parsley badgered me until I told her the owner's name.

"Baxter," I whispered. "I took him to Jody Baxter so he wouldn't mind so much about Flag."

The reason I had whispered was so our parents wouldn't hear, but Parsley wasn't concerned about things like that. "Then you're the one who took the bookmark! Jeesum, Owen, you're a real sneak!"

I tried to shut her up, but nobody shuts Parsley up when she gets going. "I hate you!" she said, practically spitting the words out, she was so mad. "I hate all of you! There's no way Owen's going to be my brother. I'll take my cats to a place where you'll never find me, and I'm never coming back!"

She left the room, of course. There's nothing you can do except leave, after an exit line like that. I was on the point of leaving, too, when I wrinkled up my nose and sniffed. I had noticed a weird smell for the last few minutes, but there had been too much going on to wonder why.

Uncle Jack sniffed too. "Have you got something in the oven?" he asked Nan-Ellen.

Her face went back to normal for a moment.

"I've made comfrey quiche to serve at the reception tomorrow. That's my surprise!"

Uncle Jack's voice grew even colder than when he had read Parsley's plan. "I'm surprised. Will that do, or do I also have to eat it?"

I could hardly blame Nan-Ellen for bursting into tears. Comfrey quiche sounded repulsive, but Uncle Jack didn't have to say so.

"You *are* a bully!" I told him in the usual high-pitched warble that happens when I get upset. "Can't you at least be polite?"

Uncle Jack made a snorting noise and slammed out one door. Nan-Ellen made a sobbing noise and slammed out the other. Alone in the middle is not the greatest place to be, so I went off to bed. Tomorrow I'd try to work things out with Parsley. Maybe she'd stop hating me when I told her that our parents were splitting up.

⇥⇥ *Seventeen* ⇤⇤

ONLY I COULDN'T SLEEP. It wasn't dark out yet, for one thing. Going to bed by daylight is kind of freaky when you're used to staying up as late as you can get away with. I tried putting my head under the pillow, but it was too hot. Then I got up and watched channel 3 for a while, but my heart wasn't in it. When night fell, I went back to bed again. For hours I lay awake thinking about the wedding that wouldn't take place after all.

Would we move back to Boston? We'd have to find a new apartment. Chances were I wouldn't like it as much as the old one with its view over roof gardens and air-conditioning vents. I'd get used to it, of course. You could get used to pretty much

181

anything. The problem was, I was getting used to the idea of living in Vermont: crazy cousin, new school, book reports, and all.

How soon would we leave? Wedding or no wedding, Nan-Ellen was capable of staying put until she reached a good stopping place in her new book. In which case I might have to start out, at least, in the local junior high. To be on the safe side, I'd better go on with the reports.

"School starts Tuesday," I murmured, counting backward. "That leaves Monday, Sunday, and tomorrow. Or is today already tomorrow? What time is it?"

I turned on the light to see the clock. Only eleven; it felt like much later, but I wasn't sleepy. The more I tried to relax, the more I worried. Would they get married or wouldn't they? Would we move or not? Would I be able to write four reports in just three days? Maybe—if I wrote about the characters I'd met with the bookmark. Alice and the Mad Hatter, and Georgie's mother. I drew the line at the March girls, though. No way was I going to be known in a new school as the boy who wrote his summer book report on *Little Women*.

I sat up in bed, abandoning my attempt to sleep. How about *The Yearling*? It was over four hundred pages long, and I had read only one chapter. Still, I figured I already knew more about the book than most other kids. Maybe even more than the teacher! I could fill pages just describing how Jody felt about Flag. And my last report could be on *The Twenty-One Balloons*.

If I couldn't sleep, I might as well read. But where had I left the book? Nowhere in my room, for sure. Had Parsley borrowed it?

"Brat!" I said aloud. "Stubborn little brat!"

All the same, I felt a little guilty about Parsley. Nan-Ellen was right; all this had been hard on her. She might be a brat, but that didn't mean I had to make things harder. Tomorrow I'd try to make peace. Meanwhile, I'd sneak into her room and borrow back *The Twenty-One Balloons*.

Except it wasn't there. Not in her bookcase. Not on the floor, or on the bedside table, or the bed. Parsley wasn't there either. Had she had trouble sleeping too? It was a good thing I had taken her bookmark—I wouldn't put it past her to go into *The Twenty-One Balloons* on the sly.

Straining my ears, I heard noises coming from the kitchen. A solid thunk as someone closed the refrigerator door, and the clatter of flatware on a plate. Good thinking, Parsley! Neither one of us had eaten dinner. Maybe that's why I couldn't get to sleep. I was hungry too. Hungry for real food, not gourds or comfrey. And if I so much as looked at another peanut-butter sandwich, I would puke!

183

It wasn't Parsley in the kitchen, though. It was Uncle Jack and Nan-Ellen. They looked a little weird when I walked in. I figured they'd been fighting some more, but I was too hungry to leave again.

"Hey!" I said, trying to play it cool. "Don't mind me. I'm just feeding the old tapeworm."

Uncle Jack was feeding a tapeworm too. His plate was heaped with some unappealing green globs that he stuffed into his mouth as fast as he could swallow.

"Bite?" he offered, poking his fork at me.

I shook my head *before* asking what it was. I've learned the hard way that if you ask first and say no after, they make you try it anyway.

"It's your mother's comfrey quiche," Uncle Jack said in answer to my question. "Next time, I'll trust her. It's nowhere near as bad as it looks and smells!"

I expected Nan-Ellen to explode at this backhanded compliment. Instead, she smiled. "Don't worry, I won't inflict it on our guests."

This stopped me short in my tracks. "Guests? You mean you're still getting married tomorrow?"

They both laughed as if I'd said the funniest thing in the world. The answer was obviously "yes," though. Otherwise they wouldn't have put their arms around each other.

Hugging embarrasses me, unless I'm personally involved. Going to the pantry cupboard, I rummaged around with my back to them until I could hear Uncle Jack's fork hitting the plate again. Meanwhile, I found a can of meatballs. They looked so comfortingly normal that I didn't bother to heat them up. I just ate them out of the can.

"So we don't have to move out or anything?" I asked casually.

At least, I thought I was being casual. But they must have sensed panic, because I got this whole song and dance about how a little tension is a normal part of adjustment to a new relationship, especially before a wedding. Tension! They acted as if there had never been a fight, which was fine by me. I wasn't about to remind them.

"So I guess I'd better write those book reports after all," I said as soon as I could get a word in edgewise.

They went into convulsions all over again. This was apparently my day for being funny!

"It's no joke," I told Nan-Ellen. "I'd like to see you turn out four reports in just three days, and you're a writer. I'm not even a reader. I'm hooked on *The Twenty-One Balloons*, though. Those diamond mines are wild! The families who lived there must have been millionaires."

"They were," she agreed, "but you can stop

drooling. Riches don't necessarily make people happy."

"Are you kidding? They live in fabulous houses on this gorgeous estate on Krakatoa, and all they do as far as I've read is go for balloon rides and eat gourmet meals."

Uncle Jack's eyes gleamed. "It sounds like the life for me! I don't know about that volcano, though. Was it an active one, or was it dormant?"

"Active," I told him. "I think there's an eruption at the end, only I haven't read that far."

"Don't you guys know your history?" Nan-Ellen asked. "The eruption of Krakatoa was the biggest blowup of all times!"

"Was anybody hurt?"

She gave a snort of laughter. Then she apologized. "Sorry, Owen. It's not a joking matter. What with the explosion and tidal waves and all, there must have been thousands of casualties. Villages were destroyed on islands hundreds of miles away. But the real Krakatoa was uninhabited, as far as anyone knows. The families in the book were a figment of the author's imagination. Which reminds me—"

She left the kitchen for a moment and came back with two books: *The Yearling* and *The Twenty-One Balloons*. "You left these in the shed. You left the light on too; that's how we happened to go out.

What did you do with all those cats—just let them go?"

"Cats?"

"The cages are empty," she explained. "Maybe Parsley moved them again."

My mind shifted into high gear. Parsley wasn't in her room. The cats were gone. The light had been left on in the shed. Not by me, for sure; when Nan-Ellen and I were talking in there, it was mid-afternoon. What did it all add up to?

Parsley must have gone out to the shed and found the bookmark! The last time I had used it was to take the pony to the Baxter farm. Had she followed my example with the cats? It was a dumb idea—the Baxters were the last people to be able to feed all fourteen of them. Opening *The Yearling*, I riffled quickly through the pages to find the part where she went in. But I didn't find the bookmark. Not even when I looked a second time.

"What's the matter?" Nan-Ellen asked. "You look worried."

I tried to keep my voice steady, to state my problem in a careless way. "Nothing. It's just I left a bookmark in here. Next to page four-oh-eight."

How come everything I said made her laugh that night? I used to want her to think I was funny like the kids she wrote about. Now I wished she'd take me seriously.

"What's the big joke?"

"If you know which page it was marking, why do you need it?" Nan-Ellen reached into her pocket. "Here it is. It was in *The Twenty-One Balloons*, by the way. So much for your perfect memory!"

I was silent for a moment, forcing myself to concentrate on the sequence of events that afternoon. I had gone into the shed with both books. Next I'd had that conversation with my mother. After she left the shed, I took the pony to Jody Baxter. Then what? I'd gone for a swim. A quick one, without the books. That bookmark should have stayed in *The Yearling*. Only Parsley herself could have switched it to *The Twenty-One Balloons*.

"Where?" I demanded.

"What do you mean, where?"

"Where in the book? Why did you take it out? It was there for a reason!"

Uncle Jack came to her rescue. "I'm the one who took it out. Sorry, Owen, but I didn't know it was important. I noticed that it advertised the Summer Reading Marathon, and we had just been discussing Parsley."

"What about Parsley?"

"The fact that she's been retreating into books. At the rate she was going, she ought to win the thing. But thank God it's over!"

He was going too fast for me. "I wouldn't call it

retreating, exactly. And she says she's not going to win, because she only read three of them all the way through. Anyway, what do you mean by 'over'?"

"Finished," said Uncle Jack. "Look at the rules on the back. It says July first through August thirty-first."

I had completely forgotten about that deadline. If the marathon was over, did it mean the book-mark wouldn't work anymore? But Parsley was inside *The Twenty-One Balloons*! How would she get out?

"It says 'through,' right?" I asked in a panic. "That means the marathon doesn't really end until September first."

I got my last laugh of the evening from my mother, who pointed at the clock. "It's eleven fifty-one, sweetheart. How many books can she read in nine minutes?"

⊰⊰Eighteen⊱⊱

IF ONLY UNCLE JACK HAD LEFT the bookmark inside *The Twenty-One Balloons*! At least then I'd know the page where Parsley intended to leave again. Or had her intention been to stay? *"I'll take my cats to a place where you'll never find me, and I'm never coming back!"*

She couldn't have known how dangerous that place would be, or she would have taken the cats into a safer story. I hadn't read as far as the eruption, so I wasn't sure how the story finished. A boat rescued the professor from the Atlantic Ocean—I knew that much from the first chapter. But what about the twenty families—were they killed?

It was 11:53 by the time I got up to my room

with the book and shut the door. In spite of my rising panic, I forced myself to spend five precious minutes finding out what happens at the end. There was no doubt about an eruption; I found a picture of a house crumbling, and another of the volcano itself, belching rocks and fire. Hovering over the crater was a platform suspended from balloons. The author had drawn a bunch of tiny figures on the platform, so at least those families got away, but what about Parsley and her cats—would they get away too? If not, was it too late for me to go in and save them?

Where had Parsley gone in, I wondered? The eruption doesn't begin until the fourth day of the professor's visit. Since she couldn't have known about it, she must have gone in earlier. But which day: the first, second or third? The first day begins at chapter 5, but that was a hundred pages from the eruption.

"You're gone for as long as it takes to read that much," Parsley had explained. It would take me forever to read a hundred pages. I'd be gone until long after midnight, anyway. But after midnight, it would be September first. No more Marathon. Maybe no more Parsley.

In chapter 8, another illustration caught my eye. It showed a grassy shore, some palm trees, and a calm stretch of ocean. If Parsley was choosing for her cats, surely she'd go in there. Then I changed my mind. Choose for her cats? Not Parsley! Parsley would choose for herself.

Flipping back, I found a picture of the professor in the diamond mine, just after he came to the island. Maybe that's where she went in! But a new problem struck me. If I went in there but Parsley had gone in later, would I ever catch up with her? Would she and her cats blow up with Krakatoa on the fourth day of the professor's visit while I was still living through the first?

Only two minutes left. "Quit wasting time," I told myself. "Just go!"

Making sure I still had a safe exit, I placed the bookmark at page 161. This is just before the professor makes his last-minute getaway. If I stayed any longer, I might be killed. My voice shook as I read aloud: *"I threw away my bucket, turned, and ran through the village for the platform—"*

Ran, and stumbled, and picked myself up to run some more. Ominous rumbles came from the mountain, and I kept hearing the crash of falling palm trees. It was broad daylight; over my head was a clear blue sky. But I was much more frightened than that night in Iceland when I could see sprays of fire in the sky. Under my feet, the green lawn heaved like crazy, as if the whole earth were a bucking bronco. Soon I gave in and began to crawl.

192

Suddenly I heard a burst of splintering glass. I knew what that was: the crystal Krakatoan house! In the book, it's the last thing that is destroyed before the platform takes off. I looked up just in time to see the professor being hauled on board. Where was Parsley?

Already, the platform was straining at its connections. "Wait!" I screamed. "Don't go yet!"

No one heard me. No one *could* have heard me over the noise from the volcano. It was much louder now, and the ground lurched, making me fall once more. Lying there terrified, I caught one last glimpse of the platform as it rose and moved away. There was a crowd of people on it: men in striped trousers, children in party clothes, and women in long dresses like the ones the March girls wore. It was the scene that the artist had drawn, except for one thing: There were cats among this crowd, and there had been none in the book.

Higher and higher the platform rose, until it vanished into the ash-thickened air. A cold chill of fear spread through me. How much time did I have left before the final explosion that wiped Krakatoa off the face of the earth? How much time did I have left at home? Was it after midnight?

My thoughts were interrupted when the billowing lawn rolled me over several times. One thing was certain: Unless I found a safe place to wait, I didn't stand a chance. So I dragged myself toward the mountain, remembering from the book that in the diamond mine, the ground never moves at all. The going was slow. Slow and scary! I thought I'd never find the entrance to the mine. But just when I was about to give up, I saw a door that fit the description in the book: an old wooden door from a ship, set against the wall of the mountain. With the last of my strength I opened it and crawled inside.

At first I was dazzled. The sky outside was dark now with volcanic ash, and very little light filtered into the mine. Still, the glint of diamonds was overpowering.

"Shut your eyes!" a voice commanded. "If you look for too long, it hurts."

I shut them. I didn't need to look anymore, now that I had found Parsley.

"You're safe!" I gasped. "It's really you!" Groping blindly, I touched her sneaker to make sure.

Safe was a weird word to use, of course. Weird and wrong. I knew that neither of us was safe, and Parsley knew it too. But at least we were together.

"We're in trouble," I said.

Parsley moaned. "I know." A moment later she added, "I guess it's my fault."

She guessed? Of course it was her fault! I opened my mouth to say as much, but different words came out. "It was no one's fault. It happened because we were all so mad at each other. If we get home again, I think maybe things will be better. And they're still getting married."

"Tomorrow?" Parsley asked.

"Tomorrow if we can get home again. If we can't get home, that means it's today."

It was quiet in the mine. Sitting on a heap of diamond pebbles, I explained the danger we were in. Not just from the volcano; from the bookmark too.

"It may be too late," I warned her. "I may have calculated wrong."

Parsley edged toward me. "I bet you didn't," she said in a quavering voice. "I bet you calculated right. Because you're smart, Owen. Smart and brave!"

Smart and brave, that's me. It was kind of nice hearing her say so. Except what's the use of being smart and brave if you're also dead?

I took a deep breath. "I'm scared, Parsley."

"Me, too," she admitted. "But it's still a good adventure."

Moving even nearer, she reached for my hand, so we were together when everything began to shake. Cold air rushed into the mine, followed by a scorching blast. Diamonds—at least I think they were diamonds—broke loose from the walls and flew around. One of them grazed my cheek. With the hand that wasn't holding Parsley's, I touched my face and felt blood. There was a scrunching sound, as if the earth were straining to split open. Then came a roar so loud that I thought my eardrums would burst, and it kept on growing louder. We were lifted up and hurled down again over and over, so hard that I thought we'd end up smashed to a pulp. I grabbed Parsley's other arm, but she was wrenched away from me. I was sure I'd never see her again. But when the noise and the heat and the violent shaking came to a sudden stop, she was the first thing I saw.

"We're home!" I breathed, and I turned to look at the clock. There were thirty seconds left before midnight.

We were both pretty badly bruised, but that didn't bother me. It didn't bother Parsley either. In fact, she beamed as she reached into her pocket and drew out a diamond as big as her fist.

"Wow!" I said. "Is that for your collection?"

Parsley looked doubtful. "Do you still think it's stealing?"

"Not this time," I told her. "It didn't belong to anyone. Anyway, it was about to be blown up."

"Then it's for you because I'm sorry," she said, and she handed it to me.

It was beautiful. I held it carefully and gazed at it in awe. I had seen diamonds before, but they were the store-bought kind, like Nan-Ellen's engagement ring. This one was not only bigger, it was somehow more dignified: a miracle of nature, nothing to do with jewelry.

"Are you serious?" I asked.

Parsley nodded solemnly. She looked regretful though, so I reached out to put it in the drawer of my bedside table before she changed her mind. As I opened the drawer, the second hand slid up the clock to twelve. The diamond disappeared.

Parsley was abnormally upset, considering that the diamond wasn't hers anymore. The way I figure it, since she isn't generous very often, she wants to get full credit when she is. I can understand that. She was even more upset when she discovered that the other things in her souvenir collection had vanished too: the cup from Georgie's kitchen, and the Mad Hatter's watch and his bowtie. Even the jacket from Iceland, and the lava bomb. The funny thing is that Pip and Flag were still there. Don't ask me why—maybe it's because they were living things, like me and my sister Parsley.

That sounds like the end of my story, but it's not. Things don't end that easily. Take the wedding, for instance. It rained, so it took place inside. Even though the cats were gone, Nan-Ellen sneezed a lot. She looked pretty happy, all the same.

197

And take Parsley. No way was Parsley going to reform overnight, in spite of her apology. I can still count on her doing something selfish at least once a day—but that's an improvement.

Then there's junior high. It began on the Tuesday after Labor Day, and has been going on ever since. It's not too bad in spite of getting off to a bad start with my English teacher because I only finished three reports. I still owe her the last one. This is because the fourth report was supposed to be on a nonfiction book, something Uncle Jack forgot to tell me. I asked the librarian for one on volcanos; I know so much already that I'll only have to skim it. But that's not the point. The point is the bookmark that she gave me along with it.

I didn't start reading the volcano book until last night. There were chapters on Krakatoa and Kirkjufell. I read about Pompeii too, and a volcano in Mexico called Popocatépetl. By that time, it was pretty late, so I stopped to mark my page.

After one look at the bookmark, I ran next door to show Parsley.

VERMONT
WINTER
READING
MARATHON

Some of Your
Best Friends
Live in Books!
Why Not
Bring One Home
Today?

Original Homes of Parsley's Stray Cats:

CAT	BOOK	AUTHOR
Tom Kitten	*The Tale of Tom Kitten*	Beatrix Potter
Miss Moppet	*The Story of Miss Moppet*	Beatrix Potter
Jenny and Pickles	The Cat Club stories	Esther Averill
Rotten Ralph	The Rotten Ralph stories	Jack Gantos
Garfield	The Garfield books	Jim Davis
The Three Little Kittens	*The Three Little Kittens*	Paul Galdone
Puss in Boots	*Puss in Boots*	Charles Perrault
The Calico Cat	The Calico Cat Stories	Donald Charles
The Cheshire Cat	*Alice's Adventures in Wonderland*	Lewis Carroll
Snowball	*Stuart Little*	E. B. White
Picky-picky	The Ramona books	Beverly Cleary
Tao	*The Incredible Journey*	Sheila Burnford

NOTE TO THE READER:

If you are interested in visiting some stories on your own, here is a list of the ones recommended by Owen and Parsley in this book. You can borrow them from friends, or from your local library. Even if you don't have a magic bookmark, they're well worth reading.

Books Visited:
Alice's Adventures in Wonderland, Lewis Carroll
The Yearling, Marjorie Kinnan Rawlings
"A Village Fights for Its Life," Noel Grove, *National Geographic*, Vol. 144, No. 1, July 1973
Little Women, Louisa May Alcott
The Fledgling, Jane Langton
The Twenty-One Balloons, William Pène du Bois

———————

Other Books Recommended by Owen and Parsley:

Mrs. Frisby and the Rats of NIMH, Robert C. O'Brien
The Cricket in Times Square, George Selden
The Secret Garden, Frances Hodgson Burnett
Tuck Everlasting, Natalie Babbitt
Charlotte's Web, E. B. White
Little House on the Prairie, Laura Ingalls Wilder
The Wonderful Adventures of Nils, Selma Lagerlöf

Platt Memorial Library

Shoreham, Vermont

Books may be borrowed for two
weeks. Also renewed for two weeks.
Ten cents a week is charged for
each book kept overtime.